Speculative North

Science Fiction, Fantasy, and Horror

Published by *TDotSpec Inc*

Speculative North Team

Lead Editor
David F. Shultz

Fiction Editor and Managing Editor
Don Miasek

Poetry Editor
W. T. Anderson

Copy Editor
Justin Dill

Marketing & Operations
Mitchell "the itch" Harris

Social Media Lead
K. M. McKenzie

Submissions Editors

Anna P.L.
Vineet Bhalla
Brandon Butler
Jeff Butler
Wayne Cusack
Justin Dill
Mitchell Harris
Calder Hutchinson
Paul Jarvey
K. M. McKenzie

Don Miasek
Luc Moreau
Emil Terziev
Marty Hoefkes
Shivani Kamdar
Y.M. Pang
Jessica Rust
Marlaina Stocco
A.M. Todd

Publisher
TDotSpec Inc

Project Backers

We would like to extend a huge thank you to all of our project backers, without whose generosity *Speculative North* would not have been possible.

A. M. Todd	Irena K.	Nancy Kay Clark
Annelise Knoot	J Kyle Kelsey	Natalie Garceau
Barbara Campbell	James Downe	Pauline Lim
Bart Vervaet	Jeffrey R. Butler	Peter G. Reynolds
Bryan Dawe	Kim Lightle	Peter Hargraves
Cat Girczyc	Lawrence Marzari	Peter Vroomen
Catherine Oyiliagu	Lisa Cai	R. Graeme Cameron
Dan Allen	Margret Treiber	Rahul Bhagat
Daniel Merritt	Maria Haskins	Randal Heide
David Perlmutter	Mark Carter	Rob Petrungaro
Ed Rockwell	Marlaina Stocco	Scott Thrower
Emil Pellim	Martin Munks	Sean W. Scully
Eric Jepson	Michael Luscombe	Stephanie A.
EssentialEdits.ca	Michael Weckworth	Suzanne Barcza
Ian Chung	Mike Rimar	Wendy L Schultz

Lifetime Subscribers

We would like to thank the following supporters, who believed in our mission enough to become life-time subscribers to *Speculative North*.

/amqueue	Richard Ohnemus
Ellen Michelle	Robbin Webb
Joshua Lee Cooper	Thomas Bull
Kumsal Obuz	Calder Hutchinson

Top Backer

A super-special thank you goes out to our top supporter, whose generous donation funded an entire issue of *Speculative North*!

Anthony Nijssen

Introduction to Issue #2
David F. Shultz

The inaugural issue of *Speculative North* was a resounding success! In the first day after our official launch, the Kindle issue hit Amazon #1 Bestseller status for fantasy and #3 Bestseller for science fiction—both highly competitive categories. In the first few days after launch, over 600 copies had been distributed! The issue has also been receiving great reviews, including one from *Polar Borealis* editor and Canadian Science Fiction and Fantasy Association hall-of-famer R. Graeme Cameron, who called it "one king hell of a first issue!"

The tremendous early success of *Speculative North* is a credit to the talent and imagination of the contributing authors, the hard work of our large and passionate team of volunteers, and the interest and appreciation of our readers, all of whom deserve a word of thanks—thank you for being integral to the success of *Speculative North*, and for being a part of the growing speculative literature community it represents!

Two main questions arose after the launch: readers wanted to know more about how our selection process works and what distinguishes *Speculative North* from other SFF magazines.

1. What distinguishes *Speculative North* from other science fiction and fantasy magazines? What can you expect to find in an issue?

Speculative North is a magazine of high quality, entertaining, and thought-provoking speculative fiction with an international scope and a regional Canadian focus. That doesn't quite tell you what you can expect to find in an issue, though—and there's also the issue of what it means to have a Canadian focus.

Above all, *Speculative North* is characterized by diversity; this means diversity in form, content, and perspectives. We believe diversity is a strength, and that it is especially important for the literary enterprise, the substance of which is human experience. Literature is improved through the inclusion of multiple perspectives, identities, and styles. Diversity enriches our stories, and it enriches our lives.

While any literary magazine is improved through diversity, diversity is essential for a magazine with a Canadian focus. Canada is a nation of many peoples and perspectives, and we are officially a multicultural nation according to our constitution. There is no uniquely Canadian perspective or privileged viewpoint. At *Speculative North*, we believe that to properly recognize Canadian identity means to respect and represent the multiplicity of identities that comprise the nation; a magazine cannot truly claim to be Canadian without embracing the diversity of our cultural mosaic.

Diversity in literature means more than the identities and perspectives brought by authors, and includes the forms and styles through which authors share their works. Form and content are inextricably intertwined, and diversity in stories necessarily entails diversity in forms. For this reason, *Speculative North* also seeks diversity in writing styles and genres.

This philosophy is embodied in the content of each issue. Every issue contains at least one story in each of the genres of horror, science fiction, and fantasy; at least one story by a previously unpublished author; at least one story by a Canadian author; and at least three stories by authors who identify as writing from a marginalized or historically discriminated-against perspective or identity (issue #2 has six such authors).

There are three notes I'd like to make on the point of marginalized perspectives. First, it is entirely up to authors how they choose to present themselves, so you won't find any indicators about author identity in the magazine, except where they've included it themselves. The stories speak for themselves. It is not an author's identity *per se* that enriches literature, but their ability to craft art that reflects or is informed by their experiences. Sometimes this reflection is overt, sometimes subtle, sometimes ineffable. What ultimately matters, when it comes to a literary magazine, is not who has written a story, but what they have written. We believe that diversity strengthens literature, and that this is best reflected by the stories themselves, without need of paratext.

Second, an author can write about whatever subjects or stories they choose, in whatever style. Just because an author possesses some identity characteristic or has a particular perspective does not mean they need to write about those things.

It would be an ironic extension of discrimination to expect writers from marginalized communities to restrict their stories and limit their voices in this way, and it is an unfortunate fact that some writers feel pressured to more expressly represent some aspect of their identity in their writing. Granted, it would be a good thing to have more marginalized writers more directly sharing their perspectives through their writing, but it is inappropriate to force this burden on them externally (i.e. through editorial standards or publication objectives)—writers should be free to tell whatever story they want to tell.

Third, as a matter of editorial policy, we select stories on the basis of merit alone, according to our editorial vision, and expressly not on the basis of the identity of authors. We allow authors to self-identify as writing from marginalized or historically discriminated perspectives, but this information is not used during the evaluation process; we look at this information only when deciding the placement of stories in upcoming issues. If it turned out that we weren't seeing sufficient diversity, we would have to address it, but so far we have been blessed with richly diverse submissions.

This brings us to the question of our selection process.

2. How does the selection process work?

Our selection process is designed to find stories that meet our editorial vision—stories that are high quality, entertaining, thought-provoking, and diverse. A story has to get through three stages before publication, and each stage has measures meant to serve our editorial vision.

In the first stage, stories enter the submission queue, sometimes called the "slush pile", where they can be read by any readers from our large team of submissions editors. Readers judge whether they think the story should be published or rejected, and vote on a three-point scale. In order to protect experimental stories and promote diverse styles, a story cannot be rejected from the queue by one reader alone. However, if one reader thinks a story should be published, it is pushed to the second stage. (A story that receives five votes with no recommendation for publication is rejected from the queue.) This system allows the diversity of our reading team—representing various literary tastes, interests, and perspectives—to translate into our selections.

In the second stage, stories enter the short list, where they are read by a larger team, who votes on a five-point scale and provides written feedback. After all entries have been voted on, a tentative publication list is formed by using the average scores. For similarly ranked stories, those stories with large discrepancies between votes are prioritized; we calculate a metric for "controversiality" based on standard deviation from the mean. For example, a story that received six votes of 4 will have low controversiality, whereas a story that received three votes of 5 and three votes of 3 will be controversial. Prioritizing "controversial" stories is a way to ensure greater diversity of tastes, and to take risks with stories that generate stronger opinions. We would rather have a mix of stories that generate strong reactions—good and bad—than a collection of stories that are all well-received with relatively less strength of reaction.

In the final stage, the "editorial round-table", submissions editors (who have read all shortlisted stories) debate changes to the tentative publication list. During this stage, stories that are slated for publication may drop off the list, and stories that didn't make the tentative list can be promoted. Any member of the team is welcome to argue in favour of or against publication for any shortlisted story, so long as the rationale for that position is in line with our editorial vision. This stage allows us to take a more fine-tuned look at the composition of the magazine, and assess each story's contribution to the whole. One benefit of this process is to make sure that we don't overlook any gems—stories that offer something we'd really like to see in the magazine, but which, for whatever reason, didn't score as highly as the others during the second stage.

At this point, contracts are sent out for all accepted stories. But there is another step in the production process: distributing stories among future issues. During this stage, we look closely at the composition of the issues, with the goal being to ensure that each issue meets our minimum content requirements (i.e. at least one story in each of the genres of science fiction, fantasy, and horror, at least three authors who self-identify as writing from marginalized or historically discriminated perspectives, etc). So far, we have not had any issues meeting these content requirements.

Final Words

Speculative North is more than a magazine of speculative literature—it is a community. Readers are as much a part of this community as writers, and there would be no magazine without them. Thanks so much for being part of the success of *Speculative North*! If you would like to let us know what you think of the magazine, please drop by our website at www.tdotspec.com or our Twitter @tdotspec, and share your thoughts. We'd love to hear from you! Until then, I hope you enjoy issue #2 of *Speculative North*!

Contents

Bathwater Mermaid
Avra Margariti

The mermaid curses like the sailors down at the harbor, which is where she learned how to swear in the first place. She has a name that no human tongue can pronounce, something between a gurgle and a siren song. Her face can contort into a range of ugly grimaces, most of them directed toward me.

"You're going out *again?*" she asks in her shrill voice. "That's the fourth time this week."

I stop applying red lipstick in front of the clouded communal bathroom mirror and scoff. "If I wanted to live with a judgmental cow, I would have stayed home with my mother."

"Touché," the mermaid says. Her gossamer fin splashes in the dirty bathwater. She's going to have to re-run the tap and pour in fresh salt unless she wants the entire hostel to smell like a tide pool at high noon, but I let it go for now. I don't want to be late for my date because I was arguing with a mythical creature, even one as infuriating as her.

I smooth my hands down my yellow swing dress with the red polka dots and toss over my shoulder, "I'm off."

I make it as far as the narrow corridor. Through the poor insulation of the walls, I hear the mermaid muttering, "Of course you are, little runaway."

•

The bathroom porcelain is a dusty pink, the floral wallpaper peeling in brittle strips to reveal the blackened plaster underneath. The entire second floor—composed of five bedrooms—is meant to share this bathroom, but so far I'm the floor's only tenant. The mermaid lived here before I arrived, but I doubt she pays rent like I do working in the record shop downtown.

I wasn't really surprised the first time I entered the hostel bathroom, leather suitcase and travel hat still in hand, to find her lounging in the clawfoot tub. Her tattered-lace fin swished from side to side, and the iridescent scales on her algae-green body glinted like stained glass under the flickering light bulbs. This is hardly the first instance of unwanted supernatural houseguests I'd heard of. My friend Yvette from back home had her family's farm infested with gerbil goblins. Then there's Bilal, who works down at the drug store. He says ghosts blast Bruce Springsteen every night in his attic apartment at one a.m. on the dot.

I wanted to make a good impression, so next time I visited the mermaid's bathroom, I came bearing gifts: Stephen King and Agatha Christie dime novels, as well as glossy Harper's Bazaar and Vogue magazines. The mermaid tore out pictures of pin-up girls and other femme-fatales, which she wetted and pasted on the moldy tiles. Then she offered me a live herring still floundering about in the bucket of fish she kept by the tub's side. When I declined with barely concealed disgust, she cackled hoarsely. Then she scooped one of the fish up and, maintaining eye contact with me, bit its head off.

That was two months ago. Since then, the mermaid and I

have learned how to co-exist. At least most of the time.

"Haven't you had enough of human boys, Celia?" she says through her sharp-toothed smirk.

I don't stop curling my hair into caramel ringlets, nor do I glance her way when I say, "Someone's jealous." That I'm pretty and she's not. I have an entourage of admirers and an open invitation to most dance clubs and seaside bars in town, while all she has is this dirty bathtub and some soggy magazine cut-outs. Even the local fishermen only bring her food because they're afraid that if they don't, she'll tell every mermaid in the vicinity to slice their nets.

"Jealous? Please. The lot of them has been coming down to the beach for years. I know their kind. They call for me like it's a game, making fools of themselves, and when they can't find me, they throw their beer bottles and cigarette butts into my ocean and threaten to be back the next day."

I ignore the mermaid's words, but still watch her sideways as I apply kohl to my upper lids with a short brush. She cups water in her slimy, webbed hands and splashes it over the parts of her body not submerged in the bathtub. The dry patches on her naked chest look painful, all red and inflamed. I could offer her some of the expensive moisturizer cream I bought off a French catalogue with my last paycheck, but I don't.

The mermaid says, "You can do better than that."

"Oh, yeah?" I whirl around to face her, anger rosying my cheeks. "And who, pray tell, is my equal? You?"

She offers me a Sphinx smile. Her teeth are long and needle-thin, like a whale's. "Perhaps."

"I could never love you," I'm about to snap, but even for me that's cruel.

"Oh, Celia." Her smile broadens, as if she hears the unspoken words anyway. As if she knows everything there is to know about me, and she's far from impressed.

So I lean down and kiss her right then, my hands knotting in her matted, kelp-brown hair, my tongue darting out to taste the salt and slime on her lips, nowhere near as unpleasant as I had imagined. I want to prove to her that I'm not shallow, which probably makes me even shallower than she thinks I am.

Still, for a long time, neither of us breaks the kiss.

•

"Where did you come from?" I ask the mermaid when I've gathered the courage to visit the second-floor bathroom again. This is the first time it has occurred to me to ask. And suddenly I realize that maybe the mermaid is so bitter all the time because I'm the only one she can talk to. Yet I'm always out of the hostel, leaving her behind to splash miserably in her brackish bathwater and slurp up her days-old fish. Little runaway, she called me, and she's right. Even here, where I supposedly came to find my freedom, I keep running away.

My lips tingle; from too-sweet guilt or the salty memory of our kiss, I can't tell.

The mermaid's face, all flaking skin and sharp angles, twists into a grimace. "Where do you think I came from? The sea."

I clutch the pink sides of the sink and breathe through my nose in an attempt to rein in my temper. "I figured you're a runaway like me, but why? How?"

"That's easy. I fell in love." The mermaid's cheeks pull back, but there's no mirth in the way her smile slices her face in two. "She was a human girl who used to live here. She visited the beach every day until she convinced me to go away with her. She pushed me in a wheelbarrow all the way from the ocean to this hostel, where she said we could be together."

My throat constricts. Only a needlepoint opening remains through which I whisper, "What happened?"

The mermaid points down at her pruney breasts and the patchwork of scintillating scales alternating with dry skin down her body. "Apparently, she thought being with a mermaid would be more glamorous than this, because not even a month later, she packed her bags and disappeared. And I've been stuck here ever since."

"*Stuck?*" I gasp, the word a punch to the lungs. "Why didn't you say anything all this time?"

"Because you were a judgmental cow, though you were the only tenant who could stand living with me. Besides, I still have my pride."

Embarrassment burns like acid through my body. I want to say, *You've been judging me, too. For the dancing, the drinking, the kissing, just like my mother used to hate everything I did.* Instead I swallow my own inflated pride and say, "I'm sorry. Let me make it up to you."

·

Finding a wheelbarrow in the hostel's spiderwebbed storage unit is easy. A bit more difficult is maneuvering the mermaid inside the wheelbarrow and filling it with as much tap water and salt swiped from the kitchen as is feasibly possible. More difficult still is pushing the mermaid through walkways, parks, and busy intersections. Children tug on their mothers' sleeves and point at us with wide-eyed wonder. College students snap pictures of us and hold the developing photos in their hands like rare gems.

At last, we reach her beach, and I press my hands against the insistent stitch in my side.

"It's pretty," I say, looking at the honey-colored water and the glossy pebbles rainbowed under the setting sun.

"It's home," the mermaid says. I've never heard her sound so mellow, the bite gone from her words. She looks up at me and smiles with all her teeth. Then her eyes gravitate back toward the water, like she can't bear to stay away any longer. "I guess it's time to go. I hope my mother isn't too angry when I return home. I've missed her the most."

I think about my own mother and try to swallow my nostalgia back down.

"Some gratitude is in order, don't you think?" I ask the mermaid in a prickly voice. I don't want her to think of me as her savior, because I'm not one. I'm just trying to ease back into our usual bickering, cling onto our old habits already fissured and breaking farther by the second.

The mermaid performs a crude gesture, and I smile. The crisp sand makes the wheelbarrow difficult to operate. With her permission, I snake one arm around the mermaid's waist at the base of her tail, and the other under the bend where her knees would have been. She holds on to me, and I inhale deeply the familiar stink of slime and fish.

When the surf wets the hem of my dress and seaweeds curl around my bare calves, I lower the mermaid into the sea. She wastes no time splashing underwater, her tail propelling her forward. Farther away from me.

"Wait!" I yell as the salt-spray fills my mouth. "We didn't even say goodbye."

The mermaid's head breaks through the water's pearly froth. In the sun, her body looks spangled, her scales a dazzling prism. Her smile is just as bright. "This isn't goodbye, Celia."

I stay on the beach for a full hour until night falls over the water and my bare toes become stiff from the cold.

•

Back at the hostel, I step into the second-floor bathroom. The water has drained from the clawfoot tub; only a salt-encrusted ring circles the bottom. There are no fish left in the plastic bucket, but the rotten smell lingers. That and the pile of waterlogged magazines are the only proof the mermaid was ever here. I slump against the pink sink and screw my eyes shut. Even then, a few saline tears spill over. I curse then, like a sailor, like the mermaid taught me, my voice ricocheting off the flimsy hostel walls.

The rotary phone down the empty corridor rings, but there's no one there to answer it. I think about calling my mother to tell her where I am, *how* I am. That I've missed her, despite everything. Last time we saw each other, she'd burst into our family's barn where me and the neighbors' daughter were lying naked together, kissing among the hay. I left town that same night. Mom already disapproved of all the boys I loved, all the people I hung out with. I couldn't stand it if she hated that part of me as well.

I flick my tears away and splash cool tap water on my face. One day, perhaps soon, I'll dial home, the number my fingers still know by heart. But tomorrow, I'll grab my sun-tan lotion, straw hat, and the newest issues of a certain mermaid's favorite fashion magazines. I'll spend the day at the beach, looking out at the sea, waiting for a sign.

I will prove to the mermaid that I don't always run away.

Not a Vampire
Jeremiah Kleckner

The creature slid through the air conditioning unit as a fine gray mist, trailing the sweet stink of rotted leaves. It coalesced into a man and stalked to the prone figure in the hospital bed. The room was dark, lit only by the faint glow of streetlights filtering through the curtains. Cold taps of the creature's feet echoed off barren walls. It stood still as stone.

The man slept. Wheezing, labored breaths lifted the bedsheet with each rise of his chest like the tent of a macabre circus, then fell as the air escaped into the quiet night.

The creature switched on the lamp on the nightstand and examined the old man. Frail arms shifted beneath the worn sheet. His auburn hair was gone, replaced by thin white wisps. Heavy folds of spotted skin sagged, ravaged by age.

The coffee pot's automatic timer sounded, and the creature scurried off to the kitchen. It poured a cup into the old man's favorite mug and brought it back into the bedroom.

The old man sat up and looked around the room. He drew a breath to speak but only uttered a brief grunt before choking on his own spittle. After wiping his eyes and mouth with a ragged cloth, he grunted and pushed the covers down. His joints cracked as he slid out of bed.

The old man put on a pair of wire-framed glasses and looked up at the creature. A surprised smile grew on his face. "Put on some Coltrane, Daniel."

Daniel was the name of an unfortunate rideshare driver who had lived three doors down from the old man in this apartment building in Jersey City. The creature had feasted on Daniel's corpse and taken his apartment so that it could stay close to the old man during this trying time. To keep up appearances, the creature reshaped itself to look like Daniel and even drove people to the airport every now and again for the extra cash.

The old man had owned exactly one jazz album and had listened to it every night before it was lost in a fire thirteen years ago. The creature had grown tired of the album but played it anyway. And why not? The creature had all of eternity to listen to the music it wanted to hear. The old man didn't.

The creature opened the Coltrane playlist on its phone and played it through the Bluetooth speakers it had bought the old man six months ago.

The low tones hit the old man's ears like life's blood. He straightened and, for an instant, danced with the deadly agility he had in his youth.

This was going to be one of the better nights, the creature thought. On some nights, the old man was a bitter ball of rage and regret, screaming and fighting and crying over whatever consumed his addled mind. On nights like these, he was downright pleasant, or as pleasant as he was capable of being.

The old man sipped the coffee and grimaced. Then his eyes darted to the clock and he gasped. "I have to go."

He slammed his coffee mug on the nightstand and skulked to the dresser. The old man pulled out some underwear and socks, then shouldered the drawer closed with a bang.

"Mark and Stefan are waiting for me."

Mark and Stefan, the creature thought. Those were old names. When were they all hunting together? 1986? 1976? It was hard to tell.

"Where are you meeting them?" the creature asked, hoping for a glimpse into the old man's delusion.

"What?" the old man asked. His eyes drifted, grew distant. "The museum?" he continued in a tone that made his words sound like a question. His jaw tightened. "Yes, that's it. The museum warehouse entrance." His back straightened as he hopped around the room, gathering a long shirt and jacket, but no pants. "You'll have to stay here, Daniel. This bastard is dangerous," the old man tittered. "We'll stake this vampire yet!"

The creature thought about letting the old man leave the house without his pants. On some nights, he did just that. Those were the early nights of the old man's disease.

"It won't work," the creature said. He knew because it hadn't worked that night. It never worked. But the creature didn't say that. That would have taken too long to explain. Instead, the creature only said, "Because it is not a vampire."

The old man's cheeks flushed red and his eyes narrowed. He trembled, boiling to an outburst of rage.

"The hell it isn't!" the old man shouted. "It flies, changes shape, stalks the night for victims, drinks blood!"

The creature watched the old man. Stooped. Frail. Thin. Not

the least like the man who had chased it over Venetian rooftops and down the alleys of Rio de Janeiro. That man could run. And what a mind he had! When he was young, the man had found clues to the creature's origins. He was entirely misled by the foolish filter of his faith, but he got closer than most.

Then the disease struck. Fast and unforgiving. Two short years took the hard man away, leaving only a hollow husk. The man became an old man. Slumped shoulders. Shaking hands.

"I have never drunk just blood," the creature said. It was true. Blood was always a part of something greater. A circumstantial result of eating raw flesh or the crucial ingredient in a ritual.

"Of course you haven't, Charlie," the old man said. "You're not a monster." He was in the kitchen now, banging away at what sounded like small plates.

Sometimes, the old man called the creature "Charlie," mistaking it for the son he hadn't talked to in twenty-five years, the son who died in a car crash on an Indiana highway eighteen months ago.

"What are you doing, Dad?" the creature asked, playing along. It didn't change shape. It didn't need to.

"Making coffee." The old man grunted.

"I made you coffee already," the creature said. "It's on your nightstand."

More clattering came from the kitchen. Fluid spilled down the drain. The faucet ran. "I want fresh coffee."

The creature shrugged. If the old man was making coffee, then he was not going to meet his long-dead friends at the back entrance of a now closed museum for their doomed-to-fail plan. No matter. The joy of watching the old man walk pants-less down a crowded street had faded along with the man's ability to remember his embarrassment.

"You made me decaf," the old man sneered.

"It's not decaf," the creature said.

"It tastes like decaf," the old man shouted.

"It's not."

"Then it's old," the old man snapped. "Old coffee tastes like decaf."

"It's not old and it's not decaf," the creature said.

It was decaf. Several weeks ago, the creature read that caffeine was bad for people with the old man's condition. Since then, it had funneled ground decaffeinated coffee into the old man's canister. The old man always noticed.

"I used to like this coffee," the old man called out from the kitchen.

"We'll get a different type when we go to the store tomorrow," the creature said. Putting things off made life easier for the creature. The old man always forgot.

The creature had thought about putting the old man into a home but decided that would have been cruel. This arrangement was more expensive in the long run, but what was "the long run" to an undying nightmare, and what did money really mean, anyway? In this apartment, it had access to the old man at any time without question or pretense. It could suffocate him with a pillow, play with his medication, push him off of the fire escape.

It did none of these things. And that was why it came back

night after night, to find out what stayed its hand. What made it count the man's pills? What made it pay his rent, pay for his groceries and doctor visits?

In truth, the creature had been territorial over the man for years, protecting him from certain death many times over. Two instances would have been by complete accident: a gas leak in Detroit and a runaway fruit cart in Syria. Many more were by intent. The creature once went so far as to scour an entire cartel that the man had unknowingly offended. At the time, its excuse was that "no one was to kill the man except for me."

That excuse grew thinner as the years rolled on. Something always held it back. Something just wasn't right.

The creature would make up some theatrics to goad the man into believing that he had forced it to flee at the last moment. Silver. Garlic. Ridiculous iconography. The man carried all of it with him at all times and added to his list of trinkets based on what had "saved" him the last time they fought. After a while, the man looked less like a warrior than he did a third-century street vendor.

The kindest thing the creature did was convince the man that the items weren't as important as the faith he put into them. That eased the burden of the man's baggage and helped him get around more easily. Now, all the old man had was a rusted cross and dull silver knife.

"Charlie," the old man called. "Would you mind helping me in the kitchen?"

The creature stifled a laugh.

The "help me in the kitchen" routine was one of the old

man's tricks he used whenever the fog of his disease lifted and he recognized the creature for what it was. He'd wait for the creature to round the corner and plunge some object into its face or heart. Sometimes the creature let him do it, just to see the thrill in the old man's eyes again.

The creature didn't want to humor the old man tonight.

"I don't feel like being stabbed," the creature said.

"To hell with what you feel like," the old man spat. His head peeked around the corner into the hallway between the kitchen and bedroom. "How did you get in here?"

"You gave me a key."

"Bullshit," the old man shouted.

"No, really," the creature called back. It drew a key from one of the folds of its coat and tossed it down the hallway. The small metal object ricocheted off of a door handle and rattled against the tile floor.

"What are you playing at? Why not let me die in peace?"

"Because it wouldn't be peaceful," the creature said. "You'd be in a shelter for penniless old fools, robbed and beaten or worse."

"And you want that pleasure all to yourself. Is that right?"

The creature smirked. "Something like that."

They were on a side street in Jersey City when it had first noticed something was wrong with the old man. The creature had disguised itself as a lover it had disemboweled in front of the man years before. The plan was to beat the man to death right there and then, but the man looked upon the creature's disguise with joy. The look lasted for seconds too long, longer than it should have taken for the man to recognize the familiar trick. Then the fog lifted from the man's eyes, and he stabbed it with the silver knife. The creature feigned injury and fled, more confused than hurt.

Then it happened again three weeks later. This was when the creature took Daniel's apartment down the hall. It helped the old man dress and took him to early screenings. The old man told him everything.

Two months later, the old man gave "Daniel" Power of Attorney. The creature had never heard this term before. It had many powers, but this was something new. The paperwork gave the creature control over the man's life and resources, such as they were. One part, in particular, dealt with palliative or "end of life" care. The creature knew that humans died as often as they were born, but this was a new level of complexity. It was fortunate that the old man had little to his name or it would have had to hire professionals.

For months, the creature didn't know why it took care of the old man. It should have been glad that the man was finally old enough to give up the hunt. But, for some reason, it couldn't let the old man go in any common way. The old man deserved better than the indignity of incontinence and less than optimal care.

"What do you want?" the old man's voice rasped from the kitchen. "Why are you keeping me like this? What did you do to me?"

"I didn't do this to you," the creature answered. It imitated a breath. "You're sick."

"I know I'm sick. You made me sick."

"I didn't," the creature said. This was common, too. The old man would have moments when he was mostly himself again. He would shout at the creature. Lunge for it. Cry. Beg. He would scramble for his silver knife, sometimes finding it and attacking the creature, sometimes forgetting what he was looking for in the first place.

"Come out of the kitchen," the creature said. "I'm not here to hurt you."

"Since when?" the old man asked, poking his head into the hallway. Something in his hand glinted in the light.

The creature waved in disgust. "Where do you think your oxygen tanks and fancy hospital bed came from? Who do you think pays for your prescriptions and visiting nurse?"

"You?" the old man gasped. His eyes grew wide. "I thought it was…"

"Charlie?" the creature asked. "Charlie has been dead for over a year. You two hadn't talked for twenty years before that. Why would you think he would have any reason to help you?"

It watched the old man retreat further into the kitchen and realized that it had said the wrong thing.

Then the old man shuffled hastily down the hallway, shouting. "You goddamn son of a bitch!" Phlegm caught in his throat, garbling the last few words, but the creature understood anyway. The old man spat and drew a breath. "You fucker. You goddamn abomination piece of shit." He pitched forward, dropping the knife and just barely grabbing onto the back of a chair by his bedside.

Last night, the creature had cried for the old man. It took the shape of a person and forced tears out of its eyes, mimicked the wails of people it had seen cry before. It wasn't right, though. The actions were there, but the feeling was hollow. Empty. It tried for hours. Eventually, it gave up and changed the old man's bedsheets.

"What comes next?" the old man asked, slumping into the chair.

"In a minute or so, you'll forget this conversation and go back to thinking that I'm your dead son."

"No. I mean after this," the old man said, looking around.

The creature understood. "I don't know."

"Bullshit," the old man spat.

"It's true," the creature said. "I have seen nothing that suggests a life beyond this one, and I know no one who has. No priest. No scholar. No monk. No oracle. I am what I have always been. Just like you. And, just like you, I have spent my life searching for meaning. You had me, or at least the purpose of hunting me. I, in turn, had you."

The old man burst into a garbled fit of laughter. "Why not turn me, huh?" He pulled his collar down and leaned toward the creature.

"For the last time, I'm not a vampire."

"Y-You've raised the dead before," the old man stammered.

"Empty shells. Puppets. Not life."

Tears welled in the old man's eyes. "Try!"

"I did try." The creature huffed.

The old man was silent for a breath. "When?"

The creature smiled. "The night at the museum with Mark and Stefan, oddly enough. It was after I had killed them and broken your legs. You passed out from the pain, and I was going to leave marks on your neck, just for appearances."

The old man raised an eyebrow.

"You were big on the vampire theory, even back then, and I wanted to keep things interesting," the creature explained. "Then I started to wonder. So I drained a good amount of your blood and fed you some of mine."

"And…" the old man prodded.

"And you choked it up and nearly died on me," the creature chuckled. "I dropped you off at the ER and hoped for the best. That was the start of your two-week coma."

The old man and the creature laughed.

"I don't know any more about the true purpose of my kind than you do about yours." The creature scoffed. "We were not here and then we were. I studied everything from the substance of the stars to the ocean's deepest trenches. But there were no answers, so I wandered. I've been a lot of things since then, and I have been nothing." The creature turned to the old man. "But you made me something new. You made me a monster."

The old man stood and shuffled to the creature. "You are not a monster, Charlie. Whatever you did, it's in the past." He put his hand on its shoulder and squeezed. "Your mother and I weren't going to be together. You had to have known that. I'm sorry, Son."

The creature nodded.

The coffee pot's timer sounded, and the old man smiled. "Fresh coffee." The old man looked out the bedroom window. "The sun's coming up. Come sit with me on the fire escape. You can do that, can't you, Charlie?"

The creature grinned. "Yeah, Dad. I can do that."

And it sat with the old man and watched the sunrise. Because it could. It was not a vampire.

Vat Life
Franco Amati

I'm not writing this with my hands, because I no longer have hands. I really miss my hands, though. I find myself constantly looking at other people's hands, marveling at their beauty. Even old hands are compelling. I like how the skin gets all papery thin and the sinewy tendons start to show. Sometimes I just sit here in my vat looking out through my fisheye lens at people's fingers thinking, damn, it's a good thing I don't have eyes anymore either, otherwise I'd seem like such a creep.

"I know you're looking at my hands," Stan said. "You better stop it."

"I'm not. How do you even know where I'm looking?"

"I just know where you're looking, trust me."

"Ah shut up," I said. "Why don't you go back up to your floor with the rest of the movers and shakers. Leave us floating heads down here to stare at whatever the hell we want."

Stan was my best friend. I know it might sound a little weird to have a best friend who's twenty years younger than you, but when you get beyond the century mark, relationships become less about age and more about circumstance.

Stan took his glasses off, rubbed his eyes and said, "I'm going back upstairs as soon as this shift's up. You think I like working the desk with you? All you do is complain."

It was a slow day at the check-in desk. It had been years since I had a job. Alia, the head nurse, said my mind was too active to just sit around all day. She said I needed to do something. So she recommended me for this part-time gig. I didn't make much money doing it, but at least I got to see all the ugly faces coming and going.

The whole nursing staff was constantly complaining about me. They said I talked too much for someone who didn't have a mouth. There was this one time Alia snuck into my room and turned down the volume of my vocalizer without me realizing. That evening I roamed around the hallways for almost an hour asking for ice cream before I realized the staff members weren't just ignoring me out of spite.

You're probably wondering, how does this old fart eat ice cream? Well, I wouldn't exactly call it eating, but it's as close to it as I can get. My brain still needs calories, so they feed me with these tablets that they drop into my vat. There's this one dessert tablet that stimulates the part of my brain that remembers what ice cream tastes like. It's almost always vanilla. I don't know what a guy's gotta do around here to get some damned chocolate.

Anyway, so they gave me this part-time job checking in guests into the nursing home. It was mostly people's kids and grandkids and great-grandkids and great-great-grandkids. They said it's the kind of job that's good for me because it doesn't really require a body. But then I started doing the work, and I realized it's the kind of job that doesn't really require a brain either.

You know it's funny when you think of it, being just a brain.

I lived my whole life trying to learn as much as I could. I grew up in a time when education was everything. If you didn't go to college and at least two different grad schools, you were considered an idiot. Then after you got a half-dozen letters tacked on to the end of your name, they expected you to sit at a desk in front of a computer screen burning your eyes out half the day hardly using any of the stuff you learned in the first place. And then, like thirty years later, your body just falls apart, and you think damn if I ever even used it.

I spent a third of my life sitting, another third sleeping, and I can't even remember what the other third was all about. Probably spent on the phone or on the toilet or maybe both at the same time. Either way, my point is, no one really enjoys their body while they have it. All they do is complain about the stuff that's wrong with it. Well, now all I have is my goddamn brain, and well, let's face it, it's not particularly nice to look at.

A lot of vat people will stick a portrait of themselves on the front panel of their tank. I've even seen some people plaster up a holo-screen that flips through a slideshow of their best pics and gifs from their life. Always their best stuff, when they looked their healthiest. No one ever plastered up a pic from their twilight years all bald and jaundiced waiting for their next chemo treatment.

I don't have a pic on my vat. I'm trying to forget what I looked like. Plus it's not my face that I miss anyway. I miss my hands, dammit. It's hard to get thoughts out when you can't gesture. They gave me *one* mechanical arm. Can you believe it? It comes out the side of my rig. It's a multi-purpose triple-jointed robotic limb with umpteen degrees of freedom that's supposed to do whatever you could possibly want it to do. Bah! I can't clap. I can't press control, alt, *and* delete!

Humans need two arms. I know for a fact there are better vat models. A guy rolled in here once with two mechanical arms. Big shot. After I saw that, I made some calls. Turned out my insurance wouldn't cover a second arm. The insurance guy told me it was non-essential to have two. What he really meant was that I didn't make enough money when I *had* two arms to entitle myself to the luxury of two limbs in my post-corporeal years.

In all seriousness though, I actually feel a lot better than I ever did when I had a flesh body. I'm not in pain anymore. I don't get physically tired. You might think, Marvin, don't you get mentally tired? No, actually. You'd be surprised how much mental fatigue isn't all that mental. I've learned that all mental fatigue comes from the simple frustration of not getting the most out of an otherwise capable body.

I had phantom limb pains for years after my conversion—procedure, conversion, body-swap, pickling, whatever you wanna call it—but now, after a decade in the vat, the phantoms have more or less subsided. I'll tell you what, though, I still get phantom erections.

Anyway, now I'm just rambling. Where was I?

I was talking about Stan, my friend and fellow senescent. Stan was terminally ill. He had no family, and these hospital folks were putting pressure on him to convert to vat life.

We had a Friday night shift together at the desk. After we clocked out, I asked him to roll me back up to my room. "You can drive yourself, you lazy ass," he said.

"But I like being pushed around. Come on. You need the exercise."

"You just want me to play video games with you in your room all night."

"What's wrong with video games?"

He grabbed a hold of my rear handle and strolled me down the hall. I knew he liked company. He was just never willing to admit it. Stan liked to think he was well-adapted to a life of isolation, which is the reality for most of the people in this place. But I'd always tell people: the person who thinks they like being alone is only like that because, for whatever reason, they haven't had much of a choice in the matter.

"So you gonna do it?" I asked.

"Don't know yet."

"Well there isn't much time to decide."

"That's what the social service folks keep telling me."

He didn't like talking about it. So I didn't press further. I'd say it was a tough choice for me too, but I honestly wasn't given much of a choice. When you're really sick and old and can't think straight, maybe it's unsurprising that much of your life is dictated by your children. God help you if your offspring turn out to be pricks.

We took turns playing Super Mario World until morning. "I'm gonna miss holding a controller in my hands," he said.

"I know, bud. I know."

•

The next day my grandson came to visit me. He walked into my room with an old folded-up letter. "I found this in Dad's house," he said.

"What is it?"

"Don't know. It's addressed to you."

"Leave it there on the dresser."

I didn't want to read it with him in the room. I loved my grandson, but I didn't want him caught up in my affairs.

He stood up and looked around the room. The place was a mess, but I liked it that way. He knew that. After placing the letter on the dresser, he opened one of the drawers to see that my disused clothes were all strewn about. He pulled out an old T-shirt and started to fold it.

"Stop that, would you."

"Gramps, just let me tidy up a little. You shouldn't have your stuff all scattered around like this. It doesn't look right."

"Hey, look at me, won't you. You never even look at me anymore, and now you want to fold clothes that I can't even wear? Does it look like I give a shit about how things look?"

He dropped the shirt and walked away from the dresser, leaving the drawer open. He approached my tank and then sat on the chair that faced me. He lifted his hand and pressed his entire palm up to the glass like he was a child at an aquarium. I felt his gaze examining my bumps and grooves, my gyri and sulci. All he said was, "Can you blame me?"

After he left, I scooted over to the dresser and grabbed the letter with my mechanical arm. I scanned it with my OCR. The letter was from a girl I dated eighty-three years ago. Carmela was the woman I was going to marry back in the nineties, but her dad thought I was a loser who wasn't good enough for her. So when I left New Jersey to attend graduate school, she refused to move away with me.

I put the letter away and tried not to think about it. After so many years go by, certain things don't matter anymore.

They were serving fish sticks in the cafeteria. Stan called me up. He said Alia was on duty, and the two of them wanted me to join them at the lunch table. So I headed down there.

They were sitting next to each other all silent, staring at the wall like a married couple in a diner waiting for their third wheel to show up. "Shouldn't you be working?" I said to Alia. "Don't you have some crusty mouths to wipe or some bibs to tuck in?"

"I'm on my break. You just love when I join you guys for lunch, don't you?"

"No. I hate that you're always making my life miserable, keeping all the good food tablets from me, giving me the crappy bingo cards. You love to see me in pain."

"You're so overly dramatic."

The cafeteria was the most depressing place on earth. The walls were grey. The tables were grey. The floor was grey. Stan bit into his fish stick and the meat inside was grey.

"All right, so where are my fish sticks?"

"No fish sticks for you, my friend. Here, today you get a shrimp and kale tablet. Oh and some applesauce too."

I swear this woman was destroying me. I opened up the pressurized lid on my tank so she could drop the tablet in.

"How was your visit with Jake?" Stan asked.

"Jake's a little shit. He brought me a letter, though. I don't know what to make of it. Maybe you guys can tell me what you think."

That's when I told them all about Carmela. I described how she was my first love and how she broke my heart by not moving away with me. I told them how a year later she married this lawyer and had a bunch of kids.

"What did the letter say?" Alia asked.

"Well, the letter was dated four years after we stopped talking. She said she missed me, that she was still in love with me. She said her father was the one who talked her into breaking up and that it was the biggest mistake she ever made. She said she was getting divorced and wanted to talk to me. In the last line, she asked if I ever thought about getting back together."

Stan put down his fish stick. "And you're reading this letter today for the first time?"

"She didn't have my new address back then. I was trying to go no-contact so I could get over her. She must've sent it to my parents hoping they'd give it to me. They never said anything about the letter. Then my son moved into that house after they died, and he either never found the letter or didn't care enough to show it to me."

"I can't believe your family would keep that from you," Alia said, wiping the palm shaped smudge off my glass with a napkin.

"I can," I said.

Just like that our lunch was cut short by the emergency alert system. Over the intercom we heard the announcement for a Code Blue: Unresponsive Person, third floor lounge.

The non-vat residents always panicked whenever there was a code. There was always someone dying somewhere, and they'd freak out every time. The floaters, on the other hand, were always as cool as cucumbers. It's probably because we had already died, sort of. When you don't have a heart to beat out of your chest or lungs to hyperventilate, you don't panic the way you used to.

The person who died was Stan's hallway neighbor. We watched them move the guy out on a stretcher. I saw it in Stan's face. He knew his time was coming. He was worried about his decision.

"Hey kid, don't stress about it," I said.

"Can you stop calling me kid? I'm eighty-five years old."

"You still have a body that works, so to me you're a kid."

"It won't work for much longer."

"Listen, whether you stay or go, it makes no difference, really."

"So you're saying you won't miss me?"

"Oh, I'll miss you. I just mean in the grand scheme of things, it won't matter."

"But if I don't stay, I'll never get to see those awesome synthetic bodies that everyone insists are right around the corner."

"Psh, they always hype up the next technological breakthrough. Twenty years ago everyone was just as excited about this soup jar I'm floating in. Life extension is a loser's game. The thing is, we just go from one shell to the next until we're brave enough to say that's enough. If you're ready to go now, then you're ready to go now. I won't hold you back."

"I can't leave you now, old man. We have a mission to go on."

He was referring to my latest quest for my long lost love,

Carmela. It became a thing, even though I didn't want it to. Vat love. Shit, was it still possible?

There was only one way to find out. Alia granted us access to her medical database to search for Carmela. Finding her was easy. I was relieved to hear that she was still alive. She too lived in senior housing, except her location was in South Jersey.

"Are you sure you want to take the trip with me?" I asked Stan.

"How else are you gonna get there? You got any other friends I don't know about?"

"Ass."

"You should call first," he said. "We can't just show up there."

He was right. So I called her residence. The attendant on the phone was polite and informative about Carmela's current state. "She's good. But since her, um, procedure, she hasn't really been herself."

"Ah." She's in a vat too, I thought.

"It's put a real strain on her family. They're not used to seeing her like this."

"It is an adjustment. Well, please inform her that her old friend Marv is coming to see her to catch up. Oh and tell her, no need to break out the Windex or anything. She'll know what I mean."

"Um, okay. It'll be good for her to be around an old friend."

I was excited to reconnect with her. I was also nervous and didn't want to expect too much. We were kids back then, so I knew she'd be a lot different. I was curious about what kind of person she had become.

•

Stan and I waited at the station for the Sky Bus to Jersey. I could tell Stan hadn't been out of the home in a long time. His clothes were so out of style with what everyone else was wearing.

"I'm so glad I don't have to wear clothes anymore. You probably feel so unfashionable right now."

"Unfashionable?"

"Yeah, you look like a fool. What the hell kind of hat is that?"

He looked around at the other passengers as if he was just noticing other people for the first time. Then he adjusted his hat in the black Sky Bus window. "This is my favorite hat. You just wish *you* could wear it." He took it off and balanced it on top of my glass lid.

"You bastard."

I thought the Sky Bus would be super fast, but apparently even with flying vehicles it's still impossible to get from Long Island to New Jersey in under two hours.

Stan's legs were stiff as hell. I could see the pain in his face when he stood up. I couldn't believe he was going through all this hassle to help me, especially in his condition. Even though we bickered nonstop, I was happy to have him with me. I knew he wouldn't be able to do shit if we got lost or mugged. But it was still comforting to have his wrinkly old mitts wheeling me around.

When we got to the nursing home, the first thing I noticed

was what a dump the place was. I had figured with the alimony from her lawyer ex-husband that Carmela would've been living in a nicer place. But then I thought, we aren't that far from Camden.

The lobby was decrepit. They still had an LCD television hanging in the corner. Stan spoke first, "Is that a DVD player over there? And look at those vending machines. I haven't seen one like that in decades."

"This place makes our Saint Joel's look like a palace," I said.

The front desk was staffed by a simple robot wearing a rubber Yoda mask. From under the mask a tattered USB cord fed into a vintage Amazon Echo.

"Hello. Welcome to Saint Springsteen's Residence for the Aging and Ageless. How can I help you today?" Alexa said.

"We're here to see Carmela Buonafortuna," Stan said.

"That was, Carmela, born on the fourth of July. Is that right?" she said, in two different voices.

"Um, maybe?" Stan looked at me for some help.

"Ah screw this. Stan, just take me to the third floor. She's in 303."

When we got to her room, I saw an elderly woman in a wheelchair looking out the window. I turned to Stan and said, "Must be her roommate. Wait here. I'll go talk to her."

With trepidation, I approached the old woman and said, "Hi. I'm Marv. You must be Carmela's roommate."

She didn't respond. She didn't even look away from the window. She had a shaved head with a wispy growth of stubble and a stapled incision line running down the side of her skull.

Confused, I looked around and noticed there was only one bed in the room and thought, this must be the wrong place.

I returned to Stan. "It's not her. Must be a different room."

That was when a younger woman with black hair and fiery blue eyes approached us. "What were you doing in that room?" she asked, on the verge of attack.

"I was looking for someone," I said.

Stan added, "We mean no harm. I think there was a little mix-up."

"What do you want with Carmela? Whoever you are, she doesn't want to be bothered. Please leave."

Stan looked at me. "So that *is* Carmela."

"Carmela Buonafortuna?" I asked. "That's who I'm here to see. But I was sure she was…"

"She was what?"

"What happened to her? Why is she unresponsive?" I asked.

"She's recovering from surgery. I thought you said you knew her?"

"I do. Well, I did."

She told us that Carmela had a large tumor in her brain, and she had just undergone neurosurgery to remove it. While under the knife, she suffered a stroke in her brainstem and had been catatonic ever since.

The overprotective woman was Carmela's granddaughter, Olive. She eased up a little after I told her how I knew her grandma. She allowed me to sit with Carmela and say a few words to her, but warned me that she wouldn't recognize or even acknowledge me.

"She's not there anymore," Olive said. "The surgery ruined her. I knew better than to trust those doctors."

"But you don't know that. You said she's locked-in. That means she could still be in there, somewhere. She just can't express herself, right?"

"I know I said locked-in, but the doctors don't really know how much conscious activity she has. They can tell us what parts of her brain work and what parts are dead, but they speak out of both sides of their mouths, these doctors. I can't trust anything they say. They have no idea what's going on. I don't think there's much of her left."

"But I can see it. In her eyes. I can tell. I can feel it. See how her pupils react to my voice?"

"I don't know. How much can you really tell from a person's pupils?"

I looked at Carmela's hands. It was odd seeing hands that I remembered holding many years ago. They were younger hands then, but I could see the similarities. The contours, the shape of the nails, the way they rested on the arms of the chair. It was all the same, but different. Life had weathered them, but their essence remained.

Stan tapped on my tank. "Hey Marv, maybe we should go."

"No. Wait. I have an idea," I said. "Put her in a vat. That's how you can find out if she's still there. The conversion process replaces the brainstem. That's where you said her stroke was, right? The part of her that's *her* is in the rest of the brain. All that stuff will still be there. They'll connect her to the new hardware, and she'll have a new life. You'll be able to talk to her again."

"The doctors suggested that. But they said there's no guarantee that it'll work. And it's an elaborate procedure. Not to mention the unnecessary trauma of putting someone through that whose body is still mostly fine. There's also no way to warn her that we're doing it. You shouldn't put someone through vat conversion without telling them first."

"That's bull. She *is* aware. Just *tell* her. That's it," I insisted. "She'll understand. You don't need her to respond for her to comprehend what you're saying. You have to take the chance. Don't you think she wants the opportunity to talk again? What is there to life if you can no longer communicate?"

"Marv, let's go. She's trying to tell you the answer is no. Okay, bud? We have no right to tell her how to treat her family."

"She has no right to keep her grandmother from a chance at a reasonable life."

"Your friend is right, Marvin. I think it's best if you leave. Carmela needs her rest."

"You don't know what she needs!"

That's when Olive crossed the line. She put her ice cold hands on my rear handle and tried to wheel me out.

"No!" I said. "Don't touch me!" I immediately put on my brakes so she couldn't push me.

She struggled harder against the resistance. She wiggled and shook my cart. Then she felt up my chassis for a manual release of the brakes. Stan intervened, trying to get her away from me. But she was stronger than him and pushed him to the side. He stumbled back and nearly fell onto the bed.

"Nurse! Security! Someone help me get this monster out of here," she shouted.

With a final push, she tipped me over. I felt an odd anti-gravity feeling. It was the proprioceptive sensors in my tank alerting me that my cortex was rotating and the fluid in my tank was undergoing turbulent motion. The last thing I remember was the floor getting closer and Stan lunging forward. Then static.

·

When I came to, I was in an unfamiliar room. A doctor was checking my vitals. An engineer and a tech specialist were with him, informing him of the parts that they had replaced on me.

I heard one of the techs ask the doctor, "And how's the other guy?"

"He's under. Heart attack. We did an emergency bypass, but he's not going to make it."

I was confused. My awareness was coming in and out. It was days before I was able to talk with the doctor to find out what happened to Stan.

In the end he didn't make it. His body was too frail. They did not resuscitate him. There was no family or friend to tell them otherwise. He went out in a moment of heroism, catching my cart before it hit the ground. He saved me from a spill that would have caused me irreversible brain damage.

After a few days, they transported me back to Long Island to sit in my room at Saint Joel's. There was nothing left for me to do. My friend was gone. I stared at the grey walls and began to wonder whether it might be time for me to be brave like Stan and leave my own shell behind.

•

I spent weeks stewing in sadness. One day Alia came to check on me. "Not now," I said. "Please. I want to be alone."

She walked up to me and put her hand on my shoulder. "You have a visitor."

"Just tell Jake I'm not feeling myself today. He'll understand."

"It's not Jake. Trust me. You'll want to see who it is."

I heard the acceleration sound of a vat rig speeding towards the room. I put mine in gear and zipped to the doorway to see who it was. I couldn't believe it. Carmela! And the photo displayed on the front of her vat was one from when she was twenty years old, back when we were still together.

"Carmela, it's you!" I stopped so that we were face-to-face. If I still had a face, I bet it would've been flushed.

"Hello, Marvin. It's nice to see you again. You look good."

•

They say there's nothing like young love. But no one ever talks about old love. Or better yet, vat love. Sure it's nice to kiss and hold hands and have sex. But the best, most uplifting kind of love is the kind where there are no bodies required.

Carmela and I were officially back together. We talked and talked every day. We played video games together and read to each other. We took evening strolls. We even took our ice cream tablets at the same time. Often we'd just sit together quietly, not needing to say a single word. And just when I thought things couldn't get any better, Alia dropped in one afternoon with some unbelievable news.

"Here," she said, handing me a brochure. "So I talked to Carmela's granddaughter who has some connections. We were able to pull some strings with the insurance company. Take a look at your new rig."

"Two arms!"

"Still think all I do is make your life miserable?"

"Nah. You're okay, kid. You're okay."

Turtle Hatchlings
Victoria Feistner

I've heard ghosts all my life, of course. But until the old woman crashed through the latticework to disappear through the floor, I'd never *seen* one.

I touch tentative fingertips to the polished strip of cedar. The wood doesn't feel any warmer or cooler than its neighbours. "Problem?" floats a voice from the nearby room, as smoke trails from Grandmama's pipe.

"Only a ghost," I reply, straightening. "Grandmother."

A barking cough. "Never mind it, then. Come and rub my shoulders."

"Yes, Grandmother."

At night I slip from my blankets, padding silently through the long house. Around me is the symphony of insomnia: snores and snuffling, creaking of ancient timbres settling with the coolness of autumn night. Crickets chirping. An owl hoots, and I crouch over the board, looking for a sign. Any difference in this spirit-touched board from its equally well-worn neighbours. I toss my braid over my shoulder twice to keep it out of the way. I will pry the board up with my fingernails if I must.

<She appears to be looking for something hidden.>

Ghost voices have a buzz, like a fly landing on my exposed neck. A tickle and a far-away quality, as if I am crouched with my ear against the plaster walls of the storehouse, listening to Father's conversations with his men.

<I wonder what she's looking for.>

I sit back on my heels, shivering from the drafts in only my nightdress. Soon the rough men will need to prep the house for winter, piling straw and stones high against the lean-tos that will cover the verandas.

<Perhaps a child's treasure trove?>

Me? A child? I am 14, a woman, wearing an adult's long and complicated garments and already betrothed. In my indignation I spot them—yes, a pair—hovering out of a corner of the sliding door. A man and a woman. Their white death garments must have come loose, no longer swaddling them but hanging freely in the afterlife. The man has his back to me but the woman does not. I do not know her. She is about my mother's age.

<She's looking at us!>

<She cannot possibly. She is watching a spider or something similar. A coincidence.>

<She's *looking* at us.>

<You are mistaken. She cannot see us, it doesn't work that way. And now we must move on, regardless.>

The dead woman and I keep our eyes locked until she vanishes into the courtyard. I abandon the floorboard and creep back to bed.

Winter wrapped its arms around the longhouse in an icy embrace before I saw the ghosts again. I stood on the open veranda, well-bundled in blankets and veils, watching the men return from the woodlot. The horses' breath sent clouds of steam into the air, being so warm from pulling the laden wagon. I and my sisters fought not against living trees and bears and boars but drafts instead, huddled around the brazier while Grandmama and Mother complained. To pace the porch, even as slowly as I did, was a blessing to my cramped legs. A fly tickled my scarfed neck, raising hairs on my arms even under so many layers of fabric my elbows could barely bend.

<It seems cruel.>

<We must not judge based on our standards, you know that. And anyway, no doubt she feels well off compared to the lower-caste girls her age.>

My ghosts drifted half out of the wooden beams, trailing white funereal clothes behind them, their see-through and indistinct bodies blue with death. They still thought me a child and ignored me to watch the men offloading the horses, discussing what they saw like old aunties, drifting to-and-fro like incense smoke.

Nanu called: "That's enough! Come back inside before you freeze." I was already stiff and shivering, but I could not walk away.

<I hear the faction is gaining in strength.>

<You worry too much. They will never be allowed parliamentary power.>

My ears pricked up. Legends spoke of a parliament of ghosts, the dead emperors and their ministers serving their people in the lands beyond.

"Eri!" My sister shouted once more, and the ghosts vanished, leaving only the voices of the rough men and my beating heart loud in my ears. One of our men looks up and sees me, raising his hand in greeting. Is it Sai? I don't know, but now they're all watching me, rough and well-bred alike, stopping in their labours to stare at the shapeless bundle of shawls. I dash inside, finally heeding Nanu's call.

The upbraiding from my grandmother is painful even for others to listen to. I see their grimaces and averted faces. But the shame of being seen by the menfolk—like an ill-bred peasant from the farms—matters little to me. I turn inward and re-enact the ghostly conversation. Demon troops lay at the gate of paradise, ready to lay siege to the kingdom of heaven; the story feels familiar. Perhaps I heard it as a child. Perhaps, when my grandmama is less ashamed of me, I will ask her to tell it to me again.

That night I am awoken by beetles and rats' whiskers all over me. I open my eyes to see only darkness and yet feel her presence.

<You *can* hear us. Nod if this is so.>

I nod.

<You can see us.>

I hesitate, for it is very dark; I nod.

An exhale from the afterlife. <It should not be.>

And yet it is.

The clouds clear and moonlight peeps through the lattice, dim and grey, robbed of any glory, but it is enough to see a ghost with my heart's eye. "Who were you in life?" I whisper-ask. With a name, perhaps I can find a priest to set her soul to rest. She must have been a courtier to move about so unencumbered, and partnered with a man. She must have come back to her family's homeland when she left the kingdom of heaven, making her my ancestress. Perhaps she was expelled by the parliament. Perhaps she has a mission to undertake.

My sister Nanu rolls over in her sleep, grunting, and I freeze. The ghost is halfway in the closed sliding door, her face cut off by the wood and paper. She shakes her head—can she feel the lattice?—and paces almost to the foot of our bedding. <I don't have long,> she says, retrieving a funeral name tablet from underneath her wrapping. I strain to see the characters. <But I am worried about you.>

About… me?

She tucks the burnished name-stone beneath her robes. <I shouldn't be talking to you. But I had to warn—> Her words are drowned in a chorus of unholy screams. <No. I thought I had more time—!> She looks over her shoulder towards the wall, and is gone.

The coals in the brazier pop and hiss. I pull my blankets around me, and curl back into my bedding. My mind is a bonfire of leaping ideas and low-flickering worries: my ancestress has pulled herself away from her sacred parliament to warn me of… something. Whatever it is must threaten my eternity.

I roll over.

For a moment I think I see Nanu's eyes open but no, she is asleep.

•

Scraps of paper from Father's record keeping: the trimmed edges often fall to the ground, left for servants to use as kindling. Instead, the narrow pieces find their way into my sleeves. Ink is not a problem, nor is time to keep my diary. Mother has set me to learn the 100 more practical mantras as calligraphy practice, so that when I am in charge of Sai's quarters I may make sure that he is kept in both correct accounts and prayers. But she does not watch me, staying over my shoulder long enough only to see that I have written it correctly the first time. Inscribe a mantra; shift to a narrow strip of my ghost diary to record my observations; repeat.

Eventually the calligraphy lessons will end but by then I will be in Sai's quarters with more time to myself. Will the ghosts follow me? I don't know. Weeks will go by without seeing them or even hearing snatches of beetle-wing conversation. They do not speak to me, only comment on household chores or servant fashions.

They do not talk about the impending war with the demons and I have yet to see the elderly woman ghost again. Perhaps she is another of my ancestors, recalled to her court. Perhaps, like here in the land of the living, courtiers are rotated through their duties.

I will stay vigilant until then, and learn all I can about the land of the dead so as to help. Perhaps Grandmama has more legends she can tell me.

·

Two years since the elderly spirit crashed through the floor—since the first time I saw my ghosts. I am married now, and already regretting it.

Sai is a good man, well-mannered and conscientious about married life. He will serve Father well and grow our lands. And yet, he is so dull! He doesn't care for idle chatter; at first I thought him strict, and was afraid. But time has worn my edges. I am not the ignorant girl I once was. How I had longed for my husband to be my partner in all ways!

It never occurred to me that Sai could be stupid.

He is good-looking enough; he is gentle when he needs to be; he maintains our quarters and behaves himself around the servants; I should be grateful. And yet. And yet, when I try to talk to him of other-worldly matters, of anything that he cannot grasp with his two hands, his eyes grow dull and his temper peevish. He does not want to hear of 'that childish ghost nonsense'. He snaps and snarls when I mention the legends and how they may be based in truth, and what that would mean for us still alive. He simply doesn't *understand* and is irritated at being asked to think of things beyond storehouses and woodlots and the hunt. And so I despair, and withdraw to my diary and keep my observations to myself.

•

<I do enjoy watching the weaving.>

A ghostly sigh like a moth's flutter. <You must not enjoy or be displeased by any of it. It does not affect us. We are above it. You would do well to remember that.>

Grandmama coughs in her sleep, tossing and moaning, and Mother replaces the dry cloth on her forehead with a wetter one. I rest the back of my head against the cold wall, closing my eyes, still chanting in 'a low breath, like the wind through leaves, or the whisper of a ghost'. I startled as a young child, when Mother had mentioned ghosts, but she did not mean anything useful by it, only what a woman speaking mantras should endeavour to sound like. She herself had not heard ghosts since she was younger than I was then.

Nanu nudges me and I open my eyes, straightening. I haven't stopped in our vigil. I was only resting my eyelids, but I can see her sneer anyway by the light of the brazier. Who is disturbing the spirits now with such a scowl? And anyway, the spirits do not seem concerned with our chanting but with the servant girls in the corner knotting Grandmother's burial shawl.

"Girls," Mother says, her own voice low like the counselled breeze, or perhaps like an icy draft across the floor. "Go and refresh yourselves. I will chant while I attend Grandmama."

We do not need to be told twice, rising from our cramped knees, bowing, and leaving the room with only rustling of layered fabrics as our response.

Nanu's breath sparkles in the moonlight. The cold brightens our senses and refreshes us, as Mother suggested. I clap my hands together, gently, to rouse my blood. Scrap paper flutters from my sleeve.

"What!" Nanu gasps, snatching it up before I can reclaim it. "You are cheating!" She squints to make out my mouse-trail writing. "This is not any mantra…"

"It is not any of your concern," I retort, grabbing it back to secret it inside my robe. She watches me, her head tilted in confusion, her hair flowing down over her shoulder and across her broad belly. "It is nothing. An amusement for myself."

"An amusement!" She sniffs. "You need more to do. You are an idle and useless wife." She does not mean that, she knows I perform all my duties to the household. She means she is jealous, for her husband Keyun works her like he does the rough men, barking orders and double-checking her labours as if she is simple. For all I know he is like that in their bed at night! She does not have time for amusements. Keyun is dedicated to Father; he has been given an opportunity to prove himself a successor and he will not fail. But Nanu does not match his ambition and suffers for it.

Sai is in charge of less and is happy with that arrangement; he has time to practice his archery in the courtyard and lead hunts, and I to my diary. If only we could speak clearly to each other to unburden my heart, I would be happy. I wonder if I can say such things to Nanu, for we have never been close as we ought to have been. She has always resented a younger sister as an added responsibility, especially one as prone to wandering off as I am. But we are both married women now, and perhaps things can change.

I open my mouth to ask her a question but falter, my eyes drawn over her shoulder. The ghosts have drifted in the room, as they do, like smoke, and one of them is poking through the latticework.

<Not long now.>

<No. Then the rites begin; that, we must watch more closely.>

"Close your mouth, you look like a simpleton," Nanu whispers, irritated, and as my jaw snaps shut I shake my head.

"It's Grandmama. We must go back inside."

"How—?"

I am already sliding open the door. Mother looks up, stricken; Nanu peers over my shoulder. The rough girls in the corner pause and then silently redouble their efforts.

I do not get rebuked for letting in the cold; Mother is only glad that she did not have to take one moment away from chanting prayers to call us in before Grandmama slips away.

Being the younger daughter means I have little to do in the funeral preparations. Mostly I serve as a second pair of hands while Mother and Nanu wash the body. I must stay both out of the way and nearby to help without being asked. Nanu keeps giving me glances out of the corner of her eyes while Mother remains focused. Outside the men gather to chant loudly to the gatekeepers of heaven to prepare for Grandmother's arrival. In the corner, the ghosts watch, whispering to each other over each step of the ritual, and I am glad to hear that Mother is doing it correctly.

Nanu catches me smiling, and her eyes narrow. I am not allowed to speak, no one is, and so I cannot explain. But I sense her grow cold, and angry.

We do not speak much after the cremation.

•

In spring her baby is born, a son, and the house rings out in triumph, cutting willow shoots for celebration, eating noodles for long life at each meal. Keyun struts around the courtyard like the rooster he should feel, but I watch, apart, and notice something I wish wasn't there: a suspicion across his face when he glances towards our quarters.

Sai questions me as to why I have not yet gotten pregnant; I respond with a bowed head and disappointment, as is required of me. But truth of the matter is, I don't want babies and can wait much longer before I supply him one. I tell him that if I am not pregnant by the fall I will journey to the shrine. He grumbles, but agrees, watching Father parade his grandson among the rough men, his gaze tainted with jealousy. Let him wish for children all he wants; I am still waiting to once again see my older ancestress and find out what she would warn me against.

We are all of us waiting for something; such is the nature of life.

I awaken one morning to shouts and wails. I pull on robes as fast as I can and dash to the veranda. Keyun pushes Nanu to the muddy path of the courtyard; she begs him to stop.

She is my sister. I run to put myself between them. Her face is blotchy both from crying and from where Keyun struck her. I shield her while our father pulls Keyun away. Nanu cannot speak, her voice consumed by her misery. "What happened?" Mother asks, arriving to help us, dishevelled from sleep. "Nanu, what has happened?"

The thin wail of a baby left alone cuts across Nanu's sobbing. Mother glances over her shoulder. Nanu only cries harder. Keyun shouts something obscene at Sai, and beetle legs brush my skin and mice feet dance across my neck. No, not now.

But yes, now. She hovers by the veranda so that she can see

both parties: me and Nanu in the mud, spring drizzle soaking our hair and clothing, and Keyun and Sai tussling, Father between them, shouting at the rough men to keep back, it is family business. From the shouts I gather that one of the rough men caused this, saying something vile to Keyun while they looked over the cattle for sale in the early dawn. He did not bother to clean himself before coming back to the long house to drag Nanu from her bedding.

"Nanu, is this true?" Mother demands, a trace of Grandmama about her, but I don't have to listen to the answer. I know it is true because *she* is here, watching. She only comes when something personal is happening. She doesn't care about weaving techniques or rituals; she cares for us, for her family, and that's why she is here, alone. I straighten, and stare at her face-to-face.

"Is this what you wanted to warn me about?" I ask, casting my voice across the courtyard, silencing even Keyun. Ignoring the puzzled and fearful glances, I walk towards the ghost. "Answer me! Or shall I fetch the priest and cast you out, spirit!"

<I was worried this would happen. Look what you've done.> I cannot see the male ghost, but I know his voice anywhere.

<I told you I would take responsibility. I will deal with her>, his companion answers.

"Answer me!" I shout, fists balled at my side. "I will not be ignored!"

My ancestress looks upon me with pity and sadness, her shoulders slumping. <All I wanted to do was help.>

"Then help me!" I demand, shrill, as Father's hand comes

down on my shoulder. And I do the unthinkable: I shrug him away.

"Eri!" Mother gasps, as if Nanu's shame is somehow eclipsed.

I focus on the beetle-wing voices, reaching out to my ancestress, beseeching her with my heart's longing to stay. Stay and speak to me, woman-to-woman, as I have always wanted her to do. For the first time she stays in one place, not leglessly drifting, and her edges seem to sharpen. As if I am looking into our pond as it settles, the ripples coalescing into a dark reflection.

I reach out, and she reaches towards me.

Father's hand once again grasps my shoulders, just as an unearthly howl rises up from the ground, from all around the courtyard, roiling like thunder. I shudder, feeling hundreds of hands—ghostly fingers—pluck and stroke and pinch at my skin. Then suddenly I am flying. I am in the air, above the clouds, there is nothing but blue sky. My ancestress is there with me, straining like I strain, and our fingertips touch.

The sky rushes to black, like ink dropped in clear water. There is only black, and I am suddenly alone. I cry out, but my voice produces nothing; I inhale but there is no air and I find I no longer need it.

I am dead.

The afterlife is a blackness, a void, no above or below. I cannot see my body any longer, simply a soul adrift. And I scream, soundlessly. I do not have a throat to cry out but my mind does anyway. The souls of the damned answer my cry in thin shrieks and wails. They scream as I scream.

<—what have you done?>

<I don't know! Send her back! Send her back!>

<I'm trying!>

The hundreds of unseen hands grab me again and push me down through the void. I fall forever.

I wake.

The ground underneath me is steaming, the spring sun drawing forth the rain from the morning. I am still sodden from it. I raise my head a little and then let it rest, exhausted. My throat burns like the worst kind of alcohol and my tongue is thick against the roof of my mouth.

"Eri?" It is Mother who approaches, not Sai. She kneels beside me, and when I struggle, she helps me up. But her touch is tentative, as if I am unfamiliar. As if she is not sure if I will slap her away. "Are you… you?"

"Me?" I repeat, parched and aching. I look around the courtyard. All of our family is gathered, many on the long veranda. The rough men and women too, off to the side. They're holding each other, comforting each other. "What…?"

"You wouldn't stop screaming. We feared you were possessed. But you are… all right now?" Mother speaks to me but looks over to Father.

"Me? But… Nanu?" I ask. I cannot manage more.

"Eri," my mother says, quietly, ignoring my question, "What happened to you?"

"I know," Nanu declares, pushing her way to the front past Father, ignoring the look of surprise both on Sai's face and

Keyun's. She's waving something at me, mud-stained, but recognizable, and the blood drains from my face. My ghost diary. It must have fallen from my robes. "She's in league with demons. She hears not only ghost-whispers—like a child—but sees them! And they *talk to her*! They plan to overthrow our Emperor! And she will help them!"

Everyone stares at her. I want to cry out but my voice is a hoarse squeak. I feebly raise my arms but Father takes the ghost diary from Nanu and flips through it, his eyebrows like crossed swords. He too grows faint.

"My lord," Mother whispers to him. "Is it true?"

Wordlessly he hands her the ghost diary. I try to take it from her, but she moves too far away and I tumble over, as useless in my own body as an infant. I am still speechless as Father orders two trusted men to seize me.

•

There is a window in the door of the storehouse. It is my only light. I can see through if I stand on tiptoe. Keyun cut a small hole in the base of the wooden door, usually covered with a board to keep out rats. In the morning I push through a slop bucket for a servant to take away and in the afternoon they push back food and water. They do not speak. They do not react to my weeping or my trembling, grasping hands.

Sai does not come to see me. But I see him by peeping through my slender window. He meets Nanu on the back veranda, the one that faces the storehouse and orchard, out of sight of the courtyard. I only see his back from the very corner of my window, but I can see her arms wrap around his neck. I should feel betrayal, but I don't. I am hollow. When I do feel anything it is grief: for the life I will not lead, and for Nanu and Sai.

I didn't ask for this. I only wanted to know more.

•

I wake, stirring, wanting to ignore the beetle wings brushing my face. But it could be rats. There are often rats, despite the board.

Moonlight streams through the single window, bone-white light splattering against water-stained plaster walls and dust-covered wooden crates. The pile of large splinters I've been prying loose lies near me and I place a gentle hand on them. Before they can take me to the swordsman I will open my veins; I did hope to see my ancestress before then. And now she stands in the corner, in her most ancient form, gray-haired and wizened.

I had thought in my youthful foolishness there were two sets of ghosts: middle-aged and elderly, daughter and mother. But I understand now, in this cage, how I was wrong. There was only ever one man, one woman. They change in appearance because ghosts cannot remember how they look from moment to moment. As in life, they cannot understand how they have aged, how their faces change.

I understand that now.

"Was this what you tried to warn me of?" I ask. The ghost is puzzled; perhaps she has forgotten. "You came to warn me, one night. Was it of this?"

<I was so foolish to try>, she says, nodding in understanding. Then she steeples her fingers together, thinking. <Do you know of baby sea turtles?>

It is my turn to be confused. "Only that they are excellent in soup."

She ignores my reply. Speaking like my Grandmama, imparting wisdom, she smoothly continues: <They are born on a beach. One or two hatch at a time, scout for danger, then race for the sea. Some get eaten by gulls.>

"How sad," I murmur, to be polite. Disappointment fills my hollow insides. I had hoped for truths and answers, not parables.

<Sometimes, a person will try to rescue a baby turtle from a gull, thinking that they are helping. But instead, they send a signal to the other babies that it is safe. The babies rush at once, and more and more of them get eaten. Do you understand, Eri?> She steps into the moonlight, dust motes dancing through her, still wearing her death shroud garments. She takes her name-tablet from her robes. Does she think that I can still help her? I cannot even help myself. I glance down at the pile of wood shards.

She holds out the name-stone towards me, its black surface smooth and blank. The memory of the tiny hands and fingers plucking at my skin resurfaces. <I am so sorry I ever tried to interfere. But I can still save you from this place.>

Horror grows in my mind like vines up a wall, binding and constricting. For all that I planned for this moment, still, I wanted it to be my choice. I throw out my hands against her, my heart beating in my chest until I feel like I will burst. "No!"

But it is too late. The hands have me, they drag me through my storehouse, through the sky, the fields and orchards spread below like stones in a pond. That is my entire world, and it is tiny. I scream into the endless dark.

A light.

My ancestress slumps, leaning against a wall, near her partner who holds his name-stone to his chest. We are in a storm-cloud gray room, dusted with twinkling starlight, lit by the moon. It must be the antechambers of heaven. "I tried." Her voice is no longer mouse-whiskers; I no longer have skin with which to tickle. Here, with me newly arrived in the afterlife, she is more solid than I. "I tried so hard to stay above it all, like we were taught. But how could I not grow to care for them?"

"I know." For once, her partner sounds kind. But also tired, and frustrated. "Believe me. Don't you think I want to help them too? But remember—"

An unearthly wail echoes where my ears should be. It must be the cries of the damned. Both ghosts look stricken.

"I thought we had more time," she says, wiping her face. She turns to her partner. "Go," she says, her shoulders straight. "I'll shut it all down. It's the least I can do for you. Get out of here, while you can."

He reaches out to her, they embrace, and he leaves.

She looks over her shoulder at me. Where I could barely see her in my living world, she is in full detail here. She does not look like me or any of our family, her features strange and exotic. Under her white robes is not skin blue with death like I thought but more clothing, form-fitting and seamless, without drape or weave; perhaps fashioned from skins.

"They will be here soon," she says to me, resigned, and I know she means the armies of demons that she long feared. "We did all we could to defend ourselves, to keep them out. But I couldn't leave without setting you to rights."

<You have already saved me from my worst fear.>

She laughs at me. A bark of a laugh, like Grandmama used to make when Nanu and I asked foolish questions, when we longed to go outside and watch the men work. She would bite her pipe in her teeth and shake her head, and I miss her with a strong sorrow. Why could she not be here, waiting for me? If I must travel to the afterlife too soon, where is Grandmama? And Mother's dead babies, my brothers? Why can I only hear the wail of the damned? Is this what awaits me?

And yet… <I do not fear the afterlife any more, only the bite of the sword or the choke of a rope. So send me where you must. If I have done wrong, then damn me for it. Just let the waiting be over.>

"Eri…" Her eyes well with tears. "Damn you?" It is a whisper.

<You are my ancestress, and I failed to decipher your warning. I failed you, and must pay with my eternal soul. I understand my fate.>

"Oh, my poor girl. What have I done to you? I am so, so sorry." She takes a deep breath. "I—I am not from the past, Eri, but from the future. I've been observing you and your family for most of my life, and I should never have tried to interfere with yours—" Before she can say more, the wails of the damned stop. Her eyes widen. "No… I need more time!" She gathers stars under her fingers and I begin to feel the hands plucking at me again. But this time it hurts, and I scream in heart-speak. She winces. "It'll be over soon, I promise. It's the best I can do—they have control over the main—"

There is a sound like a wagon wheel breaking. She lets out a cry, her hand flying up and out, as if in protection. Demons storm the chamber, and I realize all that my ghosts feared has come to pass: the kingdom of heaven is being invaded. I no longer know which side is which but as they work their magic weapons my ghost—my life's companion—she is rent apart. Blood dyes her funeral robes bright red—how can that be? She clutches at her name-stone, and looks to me, her mouth working with no sound.

I scream as the sky rushes towards me, and I fall for eternity through the heavens.

I gasp, and pull in a lungful of cold, night air. The moon shines full against the paper window coverings. I am on the veranda, wearing my new woman's nightdress. Familiar scents overwhelm my senses and I rest on trembling arms, my legs curled on the wood slats beneath me.

She looks to me, her mouth still working silent syllables, and then she falls, her name-stone tumbling from her hand, sliding through the latticework to the smooth boards of the veranda, before she vanishes.

"Problem?"

"Only a ghost," I reply, my voice choking, "Grandmother."

•

It is autumn, and I am young. Father and Keyun have been directing the rough men to prepare the longhouse for the approaching winter. If I am to travel overland it must be now, or else I will not reach the palace before I freeze. I cannot wait until spring, they will have me married to Sai by then, and it cannot be. Not again.

I slide the door closed as quietly as a thieving servant. Regret and fear tumble inside my heart, but inside my bedding there is a letter addressed to my parents, explaining why I must seek out the Imperial court and why Nanu and Keyun must not marry. Let Keyun be adopted. Let her marry Sai.

Outside, the storehouse stands filled to the brim with supplies for the winter. The trees of the courtyard whip in the cold wind, but I am well-bundled.

<I wonder where she's going?>

<Perhaps she is running away?>

They are my future, she told me, before she died. How can a ghost die? Perhaps she was not a ghost at all, but another demon, trying to trick me. I learned too much of the lands beyond, and so she tried to undo her mistake. But in that, she failed, for I remember.

But my knowledge is incomplete, and I cannot learn more here. This world is too small, I need something broader. I must learn all I can, and then tell the Emperor all I saw. I can serve my land not in childbirth or chanted mantras, but as an advisor with two lifetimes of learning.

The ghost voices grow fainter as I cross the courtyard to the ornate front gate. The threshold of my world; perhaps of theirs, also. I stop to turn back, looking at all that was my life, both happened and undone.

<Do you think she can see us?>

I raise my hands in farewell.

<No. She is simply saying her goodbye to her home.>

<How odd. She's so young to be striking out on her own. I

hope she will be all right.>

I do not know that but whatever comes will be better than the storeroom. I have been given a second chance, saved from the gulls. I wish everyone well in my heart, even the ghosts, and strike out for the ocean, alone.

Nominative Determination
Maureen Bowden

I was born on the 25th of December. My parents, with a staggering lack of imagination, named me Carol. I didn't object. The name was serviceable and inoffensive, unlike the labels that they'd inflicted on my elder brothers: Blaize, Greeve, and Storme. Sounds like a disaster movie.

When they reached adulthood Blaize joined the Fire Brigade; Greeve became a funeral director; and Storme obtained employment in the Meteorological Office and graduated, via the casting couch, to TV weatherman.

My name suggested I should be able to sing, so I tried. "Give it up, Sis," Blaize said, insisting that my toneless warbling scared the pigeons off the roof.

Refusing to admit defeat, I practised every night before I fell asleep, but the melodious sounds that I heard in my head just wouldn't come out right.

On Christmas Eve, the night before my eighteenth birthday, I completed my inept vocal acrobatics, pummelled my pillow, and surrendered to the silent night.

"We don't always get what we want." The voice originated from a shadow crouched at the foot of my bed. Sweat trickled down the back of my neck. I tried to scream, but my dry throat refused to co-operate. Panicking, I reached for the bedside lamp and pressed the switch. Light flooded my bedroom and revealed the intruder: a tiny man wearing yellow breeches, knee-high green boots, and a red pointed hat. I couldn't see his ears, but I suspected that they also were pointed. He looked so ridiculous that I forgot to be scared.

"Who the hell are you?" I asked.

"Guess."

"Why should I? You're not Rumpelstiltskin, are you?"

His shoulders slumped, and he groaned, "I haven't been able to keep anyone guessing since those wretched Grimm brothers blew my cover. May I sit down?"

I was convinced by now that I was dreaming, but it wasn't exactly a nightmare so I was happy to stay onboard for the ride. "Be my guest," I said.

He perched, cross-legged on the edge of my bed. "I suppose you're wondering why I'm here."

"If it's to teach me how to spin straw into gold, forget it. Needlework isn't one of my many talents."

He shook his head. "You don't have many talents, at least none you've discovered yet, because you've been deprived of your true name."

Trying to sound indignant, I said, "I'm quite happy with my name, thanks." But despite my protests, I was curious. "However, I'll humour you. Spill."

"You were born two weeks prematurely," he said. "You should have made your entrance in early January. You were your parents' first daughter, a ray of sunlight in a dark winter. I suspect they would have called you 'Shine'."

Could have been worse, I thought. "Was I destined for a career in the solar energy industry?"

"More likely, you were destined to be a window cleaner."

"What? Balancing on ladders and catching all and sundry with their pants down? Not a chance. I'll stick with Carol. It's a good name. You should consider changing yours."

He sniffed. "Why would I do that?"

"I've read the story," I said. "The princess got the gold. You got nothing. She guessed your name. Change it to 'Loser'."

He sniffed again. "There's no need to be facetious. Names are my speciality. I came here to help you find a direction in which 'Carol' might take you. We'll speak again when you learn to be polite." He vanished.

End of dream, I thought, turning out the light and slipping into delta sleep.

The year rolled on. Christmas, my eighteenth birthday, and New Year revelries came and went. I still hadn't found my vocation. Twelfth Night was drawing near. My family took down the festive decorations and prepared for the annual clear-out of Yuletide tat.

My mother said, "You can get rid of this, Carol. You don't have anything better to do. Haul it to the recycling depot."

She left me to it. I looked at the sorry mess of wrapping paper, holly wreaths, and tinsel dumped on the garage floor, and I stopped dead. The word 'recycling' rang in my ears and inspiration struck. My name was synonymous not only with song, but with Christmas. I could create this year's Christmas merchandise from last year's garbage. "I need a partner with business acumen," I said aloud.

"Have you learned to be polite?" Rumpelstiltskin said.

I turned around. "Not you again. What do you want?"

"It's what you want that's pertinent. I have business acumen, but in return I expect good manners. Do we have a deal?"

"I'm not comfortable making a deal with a storybook character who tried to steal a princess's firstborn child, and anyway, you're probably a figment of my imagination."

He sighed. "The firstborn child thing was an add-on by those wretched Grimms. All I wanted was someone to talk to, and you're about to find out whether I'm real or not. Here comes the weatherman."

Storme strutted into the garage. He said, "Who's your friend?"

"My business partner. His name's Rump."

He cast his eyes on the apparition. "Love the outfit. Where did you get the boots?"

"Bought them off a cat on eBay."

"Nice." He turned back to me. "So, what's the business?"

"Recycled festive paraphernalia. I'm calling it, 'Carol's Christmas'. What d'ya think?"

"I think you and Runt should get down to the recycling dump and grab as much as you can before they mulch it, or whatever it is that they do. I'll follow with Blaize and Greeve."

Rump said, "We're on our way, and it's 'Rump', not 'Runt'."

I drove my beloved second-hand Hyundai, with Rump in the front passenger seat; Storme drove his pearl-grey Toyota

Prius; Blaize and Greeve brought up the rear in an ancient rust-riddled hearse that was surplus to Greeve's professional requirements and hadn't carried a coffin since 1975. We turned up at the Council recycling depot mob-handed. I wore a red and white bobble hat so that Rump's outfit wouldn't look too conspicuous.

A tall, dark, handsome young man, whose smile made my stomach flutter like Mariah Carey's vocal contortions, met us at the gates. "Hi, I'm Shiva," he said. "Can I help you folks?" He glanced at Rump. "Nice boots."

Rump nudged me and whispered, "Shiva's the Hindu deity of death and renewal. This lad's in the right job."

I shushed him, and gazed into the young man's deep-brown eyes. "Hi, I'm Carol. I'm starting my own Christmas recycling business. Do you have anything we can use?"

He pointed to a windowless shed with its door standing ajar. "There's tons of it in there. I'll give you a hand loading it up."

We crammed as much as we could into the cars and the hearse. "Do I owe you anything?" I said.

"Any chance of a date?"

My stomach did another Mariah Carey, but I maintained a dignified countenance, as befitted a worldly-wise entrepreneur. "Give me your phone. I'll put my number in it, but I'm busy right now, so give it a couple of weeks before you call."

While we were driving home, I said to Rump, "You don't think he actually is a Hindu deity, do you?"

"No. He has a great name, and he's found his vocation. That's all. Don't let your imagination run away with you, Carol."

I stared at him. "That's rich. I'm sitting here chatting to a fairytale villain who's dressed like a garden ornament, and you accuse me of losing control of my imagination."

"I told you, I'm not a villain," he said. "I was slandered for the sake of fictional sensationalism. It was fake news."

"Sorry," I said.

He was quiet. I glanced at him, but he appeared to be deep in thought. We were nearly home when he said, "Why didn't you tell Storme that my name's Rumpelstiltskin?"

"I thought you'd prefer that I didn't. Those who don't know our true name have no power over us. That's folklore. Right?"

"Right, thank you."

"You're welcome."

We rented a unit in an industrial park on the outskirts of town. Storme, who was a computer whiz kid, helped me to set up a website from which to sell my products online. He made use of the Meteorological Office's photographic archives crammed with images of cloudbanks and snowfall, and he added CGI depicting Santa driving his sleigh through the winter sky. Impressive.

Blaize contributed a five-gallon container of red paint from the fire-engine repair shop, handy for painting papier-mâché Santas and Rudolph noses.

Greeve gave me a roll of white, synthetic silk coffin liner, ideal for Christmas tree angels' dresses, and a wad of cotton wool, essential for snow and for Santa's beard. "Please don't tell me what you were supposed to do with that," I said.

He also produced three bottles of embalming fluid, past its sell-by date. "Can you make use of this?" he said.

"No. Take it away."

Rump tried to take over the bookkeeping and accounts preparation, but I insisted that he show me how to do them. This was my venture, and I intended to stay in control. I worked hard on my creations throughout spring and summer, and we were open for business before the first autumn leaf fell.

We made what I considered to be a small fortune. Even Storme was impressed, and he was the fat cat of the family. My love life was also looking good. Shiva wasn't a deity, but he shaped up to be a most satisfactory boyfriend, and he kept us supplied with an abundance of cast-off tat.

The following January, we were ready to start work on next Christmas's merchandise, but first we celebrated. Storme, Blaize, and Greeve turned up at our business premises. Storme brought a bottle of Sainsbury's best champagne, and we drank a toast to the continued success of 'Carol's Christmas'.

Blaize's contribution was five homemade cupcakes. "I'm afraid they're slightly overdone," he said, "but I've scraped off the black bits."

Greeve said, "You should change your name to Alfred."

I suggested that King Alfred should have changed his to Blaize.

Greeve turned away from the burned offerings and presented me with a bunch of lilies.

"Are these second-hand?" I asked.

"I prefer to call them recycled."

While my brothers were devouring the supermarket hooch and semi-cremated confectionery, Rump led me outside. "It's been fun," he said. "I was always a recycler at heart, and what we've done is a twenty-first century version of spinning straw into gold, but the Realm of Story is calling. I must go home."

"Will I see you again?" I said.

"You bet. I'll be back to claim your firstborn child."

"What?"

I heard a silent scream from the soul whose tiny body was growing inside my own. I sent a wave of reassurance and love: the deepest, most enduring love I'd ever felt, or ever would feel, for another living being. Its power pulsed within me. "It's alright. He can't hurt you. He doesn't know your true name, and I'll never tell him."

Rumpelstiltskin grinned. "Only joking."

"Rump."

"Yes, Carol?"

"Shut up or I'll forget to be polite."

He grinned again, and then he vanished.

Restraint
John Mavin

Third Quarter (Friday, March 13)

I wake naked on my bedroom floor as the late morning sun—
filtered through the steel mesh on my security window—warms
my skin. Mourning doves plaint in the nearby pitch pines. I
wonder what I did this time, but only until I notice the
comforting scent of uncooked breakfast meat. I slip on my
Moonspell jersey and denim skirt, pull my red hair into a ponytail,
unlock my door, and head downstairs in the hope my Program
packmates have left me something to eat.

•

The dining hall is empty. A human I've never met before—who
reeks of stale garlic—scrolls through her phone at the big table.
She stands when she sees me and tucks her greying hair behind
her ears. "Ulrica Rawlins? I'm Accalia Larent, your new
caseworker."

The kitchen staff has laid out fresh eggs and *ossenworst*—
raw beef sausages spiced with cloves, mace, and nutmeg—but no
one's touched them yet. I check the clock on the wall: 10:45 a.m.
"Is this about last night?"

Someone howls upstairs and kicks at a door.

Accalia slips her phone into her purse. She's wearing a silver crucifix, an oversized red sweater, tan jeans, and brown Blundstones. "Gather your belongings, hon. You're being transferred."

My stomach rumbles. I haven't eaten since lunchtime yesterday. They'd served *mettigel*—uncooked minced pork playfully shaped like little hedgehogs. "Can I at least eat first?" I move toward the full stack of cafeteria trays.

Accalia steps in front of me and points to the clock. "The other residents have been kept in their rooms." Her smile disappears as she reaches into her purse and withdraws a vial of wolfsbane with a quick-release seal. "You know the Program has strict rules for werewolves who can't keep their shit together."

•

Accalia drives us west on Highway 401 in her silver Ford Fiesta. A net bag of garlic cloves dangles from the rear-view mirror. My backpack—filled with everything I own—is on my lap. I do my best not to whimper. I'm now farther from home than I've ever been in my life. We left Gananoque a little over three hours ago and we're now passing Pearson Airport in Toronto. An incoming 747 thunders low to the ground, shaking the car. Program participants aren't allowed on public transportation for obvious reasons.

Accalia grips the wheel at nine and three. "Hang in there. We're about halfway to Chatham."

I swallow the last of the beef jerky she'd given me and reach for my phone in my back pocket, only to find the battery dead. I plug it into the Fiesta's USB port. "I don't even know what I did."

Accalia raises her eyebrows. "You killed the Great Dane."

"Brutus?" He'd been the Bisclavret Rehabilitation Centre's communal pet and unofficial watch dog. I find dried blood under my fingernails. A half-remembered image of Brutus trying to hump my leg flashes. Bile rises in my throat.

Accalia nods.

Bisclavret is on an island in the St. Lawrence. Brutus and I used to go running every morning along the waterfront trail. I stare outside. A construction site's back dirt pile glows gold in the mid-afternoon sun.

Accalia touches my sleeve with her right hand. "Your dam enrolled you in the Program to learn restraint."

"My heat is coming soon."

"Ruthven House is a halfway facility, hon. If you can make it to the end of the month without another episode, you'll be released."

I thought I'd have to restart the 120-Day Program all over again like I did after the Irish Wolfhound in Parry Sound. "I can do that."

Accalia smiles.

•

Our first stop in Chatham is Talbot's Meats, a Program-approved butcher on the outskirts of town. As we wait for Mr. Talbot to finish with his last customer—a woman smelling of eucalyptus shampoo in a pinstripe pantsuit—Accalia hands me an envelope filled with vouchers, each printed with the Community

Reintegration Program slogan: *Disciplined Living for a Sustainable Future.*

"I get to do my own meals?" My dam preps the food for our entire pack.

Accalia nods and waits until Eucalyptus Woman leaves before flipping the closed sign and locking the door. "Like the other residents at Ruthven House, repeated exposure to the local human population is now part of your rehabilitation."

I smile and give Mr. Talbot a voucher.

"What can I get you?" Mr. Talbot is a balding man in a white apron stiff with the scent of cold blood. Like Accalia, he wears a silver crucifix around his neck. A vial of wolfsbane sits on a low shelf behind him.

Cuts of beef, pork, chicken, and lake fish lie on metal trays under the glass counter. A table with a few fruits and even fewer vegetables sits by the window. A glass-fronted freezer takes up the opposite wall. Mixed spices, cooking oils, and a selection of jarred sauces are scattered on the shelf above the wolfsbane. I look at Accalia. "How big is the pack at Ruthven House?"

"There are three other residents."

I turn back to Mr. Talbot. "Beef filet, finely chopped. Enough for four." My dam would approve. "For *carne cruda*. As a meal."

Mr. Talbot frowns. "Maybe you should make something else."

Accalia glares at him.

It's the only dish I know how to make. Raw beef with lemon, garlic, and olive oil. "What do you care?" I hand him three more vouchers.

He shrugs and waves them away. "You only need one." He heads into the back to start up his slicer.

While he's gone, I grab a garlic clove and the freshest lemon from the table.

Accalia smiles encouragingly.

A few moments later, Mr. Talbot returns with a paper-wrapped bundle. "I've got some *blodplättar*." He points to the freezer. "It's like black pudding, only thinner."

I look at a package. Scandinavian pancakes made of whipped blood. Frozen, obviously. Gross. I shake my head. "I'll need some extra virgin olive oil, too."

•

Accalia slows in front of a hundred-year-old brick farmhouse surrounded by a field of withered corn stalks bordered by a cedar windbreak. A paved driveway is filled with black European imports—a Porsche 911, a Land Rover, an Audi crossover, and a two-door Jaguar sedan. All four cars are mud-splattered with scratched paint and are at least twenty years old. Accalia puts two wheels on the grass but keeps her foot on the brake.

"You're not coming in?" I disconnect my phone and put it in my pocket.

Accalia fingers her crucifix then reaches into her purse and hands me her business card. "My direct number. Check in every morning, hon."

I grab my backpack and get out of her Fiesta. The rural air is heavy with the tang of frozen manure underlaid with creosote.

Accalia waves once, pulls back onto the gravel, and speeds away.

The front door is boarded up, so I wind my way through the cars and enter the side door to find a darkened kitchen sharp with the scent of bleach. Drawn blackout curtains cover the windows. I find a light switch and close the door behind me. A communal fridge, a stove, a table with four chairs, and a sink—all dented and scratched and at least thirty years out of date—furnish the room. There is no dishwasher. Buckled linoleum covers the floor. One closed door with light peeking from underneath leads deeper into the house. A second door is most likely a supply closet. An official Program memo is taped to the fridge. *To reduce food odour, meal preparation to begin no more than one hour before mealtimes.* From a schedule hanging on a stained cork board, I see dinner has been set for 8:00 p.m. As it's only 6:30 p.m., I stash my groceries in the fridge and go meet my new packmates. I open the door to the common room and am shocked to discover Ruthven House doesn't have a pack at all.

The three other residents—two males and a female—are perfumed vampires, rancid with the scents of sandalwood, vanilla, and rose oil. All are tall, blond, wear tight black turtleneck sweaters, and have the palest skin I've ever seen. None look a day over twenty-two. Sandalwood wears wool trousers and reclines in a battered easy chair reading a musty book. Vanilla and Rose Oil sit in front of a stained chesterfield and appear to be making crank calls with a Ouija board. The floor is carpeted in orange shag. A video camera rests on an old-style television cabinet, recording their game as a disembodied voice sobs. "Leave me alone." Blackout curtains seal the windows. An assortment of floor lamps light the room.

I clear my throat. "Hello."

Sandalwood glances up from his book—Stoker's *Dracula*. "That is far enough." His accent is thick and comes from Sweden. "Stay."

The others look up. All three have eyes the colour of glowing sapphires.

I let the kitchen door swing shut behind me. "I'm Ulrica. Accalia dropped me off."

Rose Oil—the female—wrinkles her nose. "*Självklart.* You are stinking of garlic." Another Swede. How she can smell anything over her own cloying stench is beyond me.

Sandalwood glances at Rose Oil then turns to me. "Community Reintegration Program?"

I nod.

Vanilla—who's wearing black jeans—removes the planchette from the board and the voice fades away. "A new toy, Georg?" His accent is Swedish as well.

Rose Oil repositions the video camera to include me in the shot.

Sandalwood—Georg—closes his book. "You are learning to restrain yourself?"

I nod again.

Vanilla smiles.

Georg holds out a hand with tapered fingernails. "Transfer papers."

I reach into my backpack and take out my envelope of vouchers. "This is all I've got."

Georg shrugs.

I put my vouchers away. "I'm here until the end of the month."

Rose Oil wrinkles her nose again. "*Vad fan*, you are being in estrus?"

Vanilla whistles. "The local dogs are going to be sniffing around for a fuck."

My lip starts to curl and I will it to relax. Past experience with my dam has taught me to deflect rather than confront. "Would one of you show me my room?"

"Wash the stink of Accalia from yourself first." Georg reopens his book. "And do not come down until meal preparation time."

"Would one of you show me the shower, then?"

"Upstairs." Rose Oil points to a banistered staircase in the corner. "The basement is belonging to us."

•

I find the bathroom just off the second-floor landing. Dust and mould coat the cracked ceramic tiles. Spider webs shroud a clawfoot tub, a pedestal sink, and a toilet with an overhead cistern —all porcelain-enameled cast iron. Rust stains everything in sight. There is no shower.

I open the taps. The sharp smell of sulfur flows with the brown trickle of water. After a few minutes, the water clears and I wipe the tub down with a washcloth I'd brought from Bisclavret. A few more minutes and the hot water kicks in. I can't find a drain stopper, so I stuff a second Bisclavret washcloth in the drain, fill the tub, and take a quick bath.

When I'm done, I dry myself with a towel—also from Bisclavret—then get dressed in my jeans and a black t-shirt. I wrap my hair in the towel, collect my washcloths, and go looking for my room. The rest of the second floor is empty. I climb to the third floor and find a garret equipped with a portable cot, a water-stained wardrobe, and musty velvet blackout curtains. An army-surplus blanket and a pair of frayed sheets are folded under a flattened pillow. My dorm room at Bisclavret was ostentatious in comparison, but at least the door looks new. It's got reinforced hinges, a dead bolt, and steel strike plates—standard Program issue, so I should be safe enough. A gleaming key sits in the lock. I pull my hair into a ponytail, hang my towel and washcloths on a hook, and transfer my things to the wardrobe. My stomach rumbles. It's 7:00 p.m. I grab the key and go downstairs.

•

The Swedes are still in the common room. I put on a smile I don't feel. "I'll make dinner tonight."

Rose Oil resets the Ouija board for another call. "You are coming back too early."

Georg doesn't look up from his book. "The Program mandates a strict schedule."

I check my phone. 7:05 p.m. I was sure I'd read the schedule and warning sign correctly.

Vanilla smirks. "Your fur didn't clog the drain, did it?"

I slip into the kitchen. The schedule still says dinner is set for 8:00 p.m., but the Program sign has been altered in red ink. *To reduce food odour, meal preparation to begin no more than one half-hour before mealtimes. No dog food allowed.* My lip starts to curl again so I decide to give myself a tour of the grounds for the next half hour. In the backyard I find a wooden swing set, a dormant vegetable garden, a concrete birdbath, and a pair of green plastic garbage bins. A ten-speed bike with underinflated tires leans against the swing set.

I'd like to call home, but my first caseworker blocked my phone when I joined the Program—any contact with my pack is forbidden, so I pass the time scrolling through old photos. My littermates Randall and Lowell howling at a midmorning moon during an all-pack hunt on Opeongo Island. My sire sunning himself on the shores of Lake Lavielle. My dam scowling at the Algonquin Visitor's Centre when my first caseworker took me away. I stay out until the sun sets at 7:30 p.m.

•

I'm in the kitchen making a vampire-friendly *carne cruda*—no garlic—when the Swedes come in. I've already set the table for four. I hold up my mixing bowl. "I hope you're hungry."

Georg's copy of *Dracula* is tucked under his arm. He pulls out a chair for Rose Oil.

She shakes her head and moves to the opposite side of the table.

Georg blinks, then sits and opens his book.

Rose Oil flares her nostrils at me. "*Din jävla idiot!*"

I cock my head. "What?"

She points at the garlic clove I've left on the counter. "That!"

"Sorry." I scoop the garlic up and drop it into the garbage under the sink.

She bares her fangs. "*Nej!* Is not being good enough."

Vanilla opens the fridge and takes out two containers stamped with Talbot's Meats logos. *Svartsoppa* and *blodkorv*—blood soup and sausages. He empties them into a saucepan and skillet to reheat on the stove then points to the outside door. "Get rid of the garlic."

"Sorry." I grab the whole garbage bag and run it out to the bins in the backyard.

When I return, the Swedes are already eating. My place setting has been removed and Rose Oil's feet are propped on the empty chair.

I grab my mixing bowl and approach the table. "Accalia didn't tell me you weren't wolves."

Vanilla slurps his soup and looks to Georg, pointedly ignoring me. "There's a *Friday the 13th* marathon playing across the border in Detroit."

I clear my throat. "May I sit?"

Rose Oil keeps her feet on the chair. "That will be being fun, Jon."

Georg sighs. "Mary liked films." He turns a page.

Vanilla—Jon—grins and has another slurp of soup.

I take my mixing bowl to the common room. I sit on the chesterfield and turn on the television. A meteorologist in a too-tight purple dress reviews the local forecast. The sky will be clouding over before moonrise with a ten percent chance of overnight snow. When I've had my fill, I return to the kitchen. I stretch Saran Wrap over my leftovers and store them in the fridge.

Jon points to the cork board. "Check the chore chart."

The Swedes have added my name, crossing off Georg's. My duties include taking out the garbage every night, sweeping the kitchen floor, keeping myself odour-free, and never bringing garlic into the House again—all written in a feminine cursive. From the chart, I learn Rose Oil's name is Carolina.

Jon smirks.

My dam would tell me not to make a fuss—a little hazing couldn't possibly hurt me. I fake a smile then open the supply closet. Stacked around a well-used washer and mismatched dryer are cartons filled with disinfectant wipes, powdered cleanser, bleach, spot remover, a broom, a dustpan, and an upright vacuum. I grab the broom and dustpan.

•

I'm emptying the dustpan into an outside bin when the Swedes start their cars: Georg, the Land Rover; Carolina, the crossover; and Jon, the Porsche. Engines roar and gravel spits as they race into the twilight. I go back inside, climb the stairs, and lock the door to my garret. I check my curtains to make sure I won't be tempted by the moon if the meteorologist miscalculated and smile when I find steel bars protecting my windows.

•

Waning Crescent (Tuesday, March 17)

I wake just before noon. Last night while I did my laundry, Georg lectured me on how my daytime movements were creaking the floorboards over his basement vault and disturbing his diurnal torpor. He sounded just like my dam. I promised to be more considerate. As of today, I've got exactly two weeks left in the Program. I open my curtains. The moon is up. I dress quickly in my running gear and tiptoe outside.

The Swedes' cars still fill the driveway, so I stretch on the road where loose gravel digs into my thighs. I brush it off, attach my earbuds to my phone, and crank Metallica. It's getting warmer and the organic scent of thawing dirt has joined the mix of last year's manure and creosote. To the east lies a set of railway tracks; to the west, the county highway. Both Chatham and Talbot's Meats are to the north. I run back and forth between the highway and the tracks four times.

I call Accalia as I begin my cool down.

"Are the others too much for you, hon?"

"Nothing I can't handle." My dam would be proud.

•

After my bath, I sneak downstairs for another look at the chore chart. The Swedes have altered it again, this time erasing Carolina's name. Along with my other duties, I now have to wash everyone's dishes, vacuum the common room, quit shedding on the furniture, and stop barking at passing cars. I scratch the last two off the list and grab the vacuum from the closet. I bang the first few walls with the vacuum, but stop when I realize I'm being petulant—my dam says it's one of my worst traits. I finish the rest of my chores as quietly as I can. When I'm done, I carry the ten-speed into town and inflate the tires at a gas station. Then, I go to Talbot's to discuss dinner options that don't include garlic.

"What about *steak tartare?*" Mr. Talbot reaches for a tray under the counter. "Finely minced raw beef with onions, capers, and an egg yolk." A *Happy St. Patrick's Day* banner hangs in the window.

"Enough for four."

"How's the sharing going for you?" He bends to pick up the tray of beef.

"Mind your own business, human." My dam's voice echoes in my head. It's taken me four days to get through the *carne cruda,* but I didn't waste anything.

"Watch your tone, wolf." He glances meaningfully at the wolfsbane. "I'm trying to help you."

·

I'm in the kitchen slicing onions when the Swedes emerge blurry-eyed from the basement at sunset. Georg wears his usual black turtleneck and wool trousers. He's finished Stoker and is on to Polodori's *The Vampyre: A Tale.* Both Carolina and Jon wear green—she in a polyester mini-dress with striped thigh-high stockings, he in a sequined vest, puffed tie, and a plastic top hat complete with an oversized felt shamrock. Carolina sets the table for three. "*Din jävla idiot.* You will be vacuuming at night next time."

I cringe. "I'm sorry." My dam says I constantly shit on those around me. I slide the onions into my mixing bowl. "I think you'll like what I'm making tonight."

Jon takes a package of *blodplättar* from the freezer. "Jesus, Mary, and Joseph, you really are an *eejit*. We've told you we won't eat with you four days running." His put-on Irish accent is borderline offensive.

"Don't you want something fresh?"

"Lassie, we'll never eat with the likes of you." Jon whistles a jig as he gets out a skillet. "Ever."

Georg pulls out a chair for Carolina, but as usual, she sits on the opposite side of the table and props her feet on the chair which should be mine. His shoulders slump as he opens Polodori.

I carry my dinner to the common room. The meteorologist warns of a twenty-five percent chance of overnight freezing rain. She's slipped a green t-shirt over her dress which renders her torso invisible. She giggles then explains the green screen effect should appease those viewers who complain about her standing in front of their town on the map.

•

New Moon (Friday, March 20)
Jon's Porsche has been missing since Wednesday morning, so there's room to stretch on the paved driveway. Rejuvenating grass joins the manure medley as the creosote underlay disappears.

I'm at the railway tracks when I notice a sanguineous secretion running down my thighs—a sign my heat will be coming in a few days. I sprint back to the House, clean myself as fast as I can, and stuff a washcloth in my underwear. My dam has always encouraged self-reliance. I call Accalia to assure her things are fine then hurry to Chatham for sanitary supplies. I visit Mr.

Talbot to put on a pad and a new pair of leak-proof underwear in his bathroom.

"You ever tried *kitfo?*" Mr. Talbot asks when I come out.

"What's that?"

"Ethiopian. Minced raw beef marinated in a chili-based spice blend."

My stomach rumbles. "I'll take enough for one." I hand him a voucher.

Mr. Talbot smiles. "Given up on the night crawlers?"

I nod. "How do I make it?" I reach for my phone to look up the recipe, but it's not in my pocket. I must have left it in my room.

Mr. Talbot writes the recipe on a piece of paper and gives it to me.

•

The Swedes are in the common room when I get back, again dressed in black turtlenecks and swimming in perfume. Georg reads Le Fanu's *Carmilla* in his chair. Carolina has connected her camera to her laptop and is editing video files on the chesterfield. Jon is playing Warren Zevon's "Werewolves of London" on an audio dock perched on the television cabinet. He's been wearing medical tape on his forehead since crashing the Porsche Tuesday night.

I fake a smile. "Hello."

Carolina pinches her nose. "*Du stinker!*"

Georg doesn't even bother looking up. "Bathe."

Jon rubs between his legs and pretends to whimper.

"Bite me." I cross the room to mute Jon's audio dock and stop. The dock is attached to my phone. I rip out the cable. "Never touch my stuff again."

Carolina and Jon wiggle their hands and feign fear. "Ooooh."

Georg closes his book. "What consequence do you propose?"

I will myself to relax. Their strength doesn't rely on a shapeshift and today is the new moon. I take another bath then lock myself in my garret where I insert a menstrual cup, put on a fresh pair of leak-proof underwear, and curl up on my cot.

•

Waxing Crescent (Monday, March 23)
The Swedes took Jon's name off the chore chart last night. Now I've got to do the meal prep and cooking for everyone. I'm also required to bleach the kitchen after every meal, stop burying bones in the yard, and quit licking myself in the common room.

When I open the door for my run I'm hit hard with the scent of unneutered male Doberman Pinscher. He's locked in a prefab chain-link run where the vegetable garden used to be. He barks when he catches my scent. His tail stub wags. His cropped ears perk.

I do my best to ignore him and stretch on the paved driveway. Carolina's Audi is now gone, too. Only Georg's Land Rover and the Jag—which I've never seen them use—are left. I listen to Ozzy on a double run—out to the tracks then back to the highway eight times. My dam likes Ozzy and she never exposes her belly to anyone. Ever. And no one dares cross her. Ever. Not even my sire.

I get back to Ruthven House, have a quick bath, say nothing to Accalia at check-in, and visit Mr. Talbot. He recommends *carpaccio*. Thin slivers of raw beef drizzled with mustard sauce. "Do you want me to slice it for you, Ulrica?"

"No, thank you." I hand him a voucher and slide my wrapped groceries into my pack. "I want to do it myself."

•

As I slice my beef in the kitchen, I intentionally drop a metal bowl on the floor and stomp my feet on the linoleum. With the Doberman in the yard, I don't have any trouble suppressing my guilt. I have to drop the bowl three more times before the Swedes appear at 5:00 p.m.—long before the new meal prep time of 7:45 p.m. My beef smells wonderful.

Georg folds his arms across his chest.

Carolina wrinkles her nose as she stands in the common room doorway. "*Helvete!* You are smelling like a used tampon."

Jon, who's wearing dark sunglasses, points to the food odours sign as he moves to block the outside door.

I whistle the tune from "Werewolves of London" and keep slicing my *carpaccio*.

Jon takes off his sunglasses and winces. Both of his eyebrows are ragged and held together with fresh medical tape. He tries to glare at me.

I set down my knife but keep whistling. *Wuh-wa, wuh-wa, wa wa wa wa.*

Georg's face hardens. "What are you doing?"

I arrange my beef on a plate and pour my sauce over it. "Your hazing stops now."

Carolina scowls. "*Nej*, it is stopping when we are saying it is stopping."

"Remember, we've seen your phone." Jon rubs his crotch and howls.

"Go hump a leg." I dip my fingers in mustard sauce and lick them one by one. "Oh, I'm sorry. You can't. Your kind doesn't have living genitalia."

Carolina hisses. "*Släng dig i väggen!*"

"I have no idea what you're saying." I smile wide. "But I wonder, do you have to act like teenagers to feel anything at all or are the three of you just dicks?" I run the water in the sink and rinse the metal bowl I'd made the sauce in.

Jon stops howling and bares his fangs. "Go chase a car."

"Which one? Yours are almost gone." I turn off the tap and put the bowl on the counter. "How come you never take the Jag?"

Georg points to the outside door. "Get out."

I shrug. "Sure. In eight days."

Carolina hisses again.

I roll my eyes.

Jon puts his fangs away. "Look at me."

I do.

He tries this hypno-mind tick on me, getting all charismatic, lowering his voice, and amping up the suave. "You want to please me."

He looks ridiculous with the medical tape holding his eyebrows together. I laugh in his face.

"Fine." Jon frowns. "Go hump your new boyfriend."

Carolina steps closer. "He is meaning the Doberman."

A growl rumbles my throat.

Jon smirks. "The odds are three to one in our favour and the moon isn't out."

I laugh again. Moonrise had been at 9:30 a.m., an ass-sniffingly important detail they'd failed to register. I reach over the counter and open the blackout curtains. The crescent moon hangs over the cedar windbreak at the edge of the field. I feel a slight invigoration. More importantly, direct sunlight enters the room. Dust motes dance in the air. Reflections from the metal bowl dazzle the ceiling. Everyone's irises contract.

Jon whips on his sunglasses and jumps back.

Carolina squeaks as she hides in the supply closet.

Georg closes the closet door. "Shut the curtains!"

"Get rid of the Doberman."

A few tense minutes pass where we glare at each other, me in the sunlight by the counter, the Swedes in the shadows. Finally, when the sun reaches the closet door, Georg swallows. "Okay."

I close the curtains and the Swedes relocate to the basement. I carry the television into the kitchen and enjoy my *carpaccio* at the table with the meteorologist in the too-tight dress, which is yellow today. She tells me the skies are to remain clear and the moon isn't due to set until midnight. Midway through her forecast, someone hands her a grey cardigan to cover herself.

•

First Quarter (Friday, March 27)
While the weather is getting warmer, it's also been overcast for days and the Doberman is still in the backyard. I crank Danzig on my phone and go for a double run.

When I get back, I discover the Swedes have locked me out of the House. Carolina watches through the kitchen window, wearing sunglasses and wrapped in a hooded cloak. She shoots me the finger. She's wearing leather gloves. Someone cranks "Werewolves of London" on the audio dock. They must have downloaded their own copy.

While my dam's authority at home is undisputed, she certainly doesn't do everything herself. I call Accalia and demand an immediate transfer.

"You've got five days left, hon." Her voice is saccharine.

"They've brought in an unneutered Doberman."

Accalia grows stern. "It's within their rights as Program participants to keep a pet."

"My heat is coming!"

"You can do this."

"You remember Brutus and the Irish Wolfhound?"

Her tone lightens. "Consider this your final test. If you can make it through this last week, then there'll be nothing the human world can throw at you that you won't be able to handle. You'll be the Community Reintegration Program's greatest success."

I hang up and grab the ten-speed.

•

Mr. Talbot smiles as I enter. "How about some *koi soi*? It's Thai. Ground lean beef marinated in fish sauce, lime juice, chilies, and herbs."

I shake my head. "Not today, thanks."

"*Yukhoe*? Korean beef fillet sliced into matchsticks then marinated in soy sauce, sugar, and sesame oil. Flavour it with spring onions and sesame seeds and serve with a raw egg yolk on top."

"Too complicated."

Mr. Talbot looks under his counter. "A fresh t-bone?"

"Perfect." I give him a voucher.

•

I'm camped out on the wooden swing set, figuring I'll wait until the Swedes leave for the night before I lock myself in my garret. The steel bars on the windows and my reinforced door will keep me safe. I nibble at my t-bone, trying to make it last. Even without seasonings, it tastes awesome.

Some crows land in the field to peck at desiccated corn cobs. They're beyond chasing distance, so the Doberman keeps his focus on me. After a while he starts to whine. He really wants my dinner. Or to make friends. I'm not sure which. I toss him the bone after I finish and he settles down for a good gnaw.

The Swedes don't come out of the House until twilight is over and true night has begun. They all climb into the Land Rover and speed off toward Chatham. The scent of their exhaust hangs heavy in the air.

I wait until I can no longer see their brake lights. Then I go inside, gather all the *blodplättar, svartsoppa,* and *blodkorv* from the fridge, and throw it out. Then, I take an hour-long bath, reinsert my cup, put on some clean underwear, and head to my garret.

•

My blackout curtains are gone. My bedding is missing, too—the sheets, the blanket, and my pillow. My Bisclavret towel unravels from my head, but before I can turn around, my door slams shut. The Swedes seal it by driving nails through the doorframe. From beneath my cot, the Doberman whines. I growl and punch the door, but of course it won't budge as it's reinforced to Program specs. Then I notice the large jug of water and a giant bag of kibble on the floor.

•

Waxing Gibbous (Tuesday, March 31)
I wake at dawn to the strong scent of cowering Doberman. I open my eyes and blink into the sunlight streaming through my bare windows. I check my leak-proof underwear—no fresh blood. I pull out my cup. My secretions are running clear. I'm now in full estrus. I punch the door. "Let me out of here!"

Squeaking noises like a puppy's chew toy are my only reply.

The Doberman whimpers from under my cot.

I kick the door but it barely even rocks. My dam always ridiculed my tantrums, recounting them with relish over pack dinners. I swallow my anger. Today is my last day in the Program. I can do this.

On the other side of my door, the Swedes start whistling. *Wuh-wa, wuh-wa, wa wa wa wa.*

The Doberman crawls out from under my cot.

I growl and point at the floor.

He sits. Immediately.

I check the weather on my phone. Moonrise isn't until 4:30 p.m.

•

The Swedes stop whistling at sunset. The front door opens and closes. A few minutes later, they come around to the backyard. Silver moonlight bathes the recently-tilled fields.

Carolina balances her video camera on the empty dog run and points it at my windows. "*Hej*! You will be smiling now!"

Jon holds up the squeak toy. It's a rubber novelty penis, complete with a cartoon face. "Show the world what a depraved slut you really are."

I shoot him the finger.

Georg floats up and smiles. "Let the Doberman mount you and this will all be over."

My lip curls.

Jon floats up and taps my window glass. "Get her, Remus! Come on, boy!"

The Doberman—Remus—stands and starts to shake. His penis extends, furless and pink.

I feel an overwhelming urge to raise my hindquarters. I almost puke. "Sit!"

Remus turns in a circle.

"Now!"

He whimpers once and sits. Slowly.

I call Accalia. "Get me out of here!"

She tsks. "Today's your last day, hon."

"They're trying to make me fuck the Doberman!"

Accalia hangs up.

I throw my phone across the room. It shatters when it hits the wardrobe.

Outside, Jon shoves the squeak toy down his pants.

Georg taps my window. "It is too bad your phone is broken." He points to a silver Ford Fiesta idling on the road. Accalia sits in the driver's seat with a pair of binoculars. "You could have reminded your caseworker that Ruthven House is not a kennel. How dare she replace Mary with you?"

I kick the door again. "Who the fuck is Mary?"

Georg's face hardens. He turns to Carolina.

She shakes her head.

Remus licks his lips and gets to his feet.

I have to fight the urge to get on all fours. "Down!"

Remus squats.

Jon squeaks the rubber penis between his thighs and pretends to orgasm.

Remus stands again.

Although my dam won't let others do it, she does bend the rules to suit herself. Maybe that's what I'm supposed to learn. I shift slightly—no fur—just enough to make me stronger than your average house pet. My lupine desire skyrockets. Bile fills my mouth. I grab Remus by the scruff of his neck, snap his spine, and jam his corpse against the window. "Leave me alone, Georg! I'm going home!"

Georg blinks then motions for Carolina and Jon to follow him back inside. They leave the video camera running. Georg tries to put his arm around Carolina.

She slaps his hand. "*Jag är inte* Mary."

Accalia drives away.

•

Full Moon (Saturday, April 4)

I've been locked in my garret with a dead dog and no toilet for five days. It reeks in here. I finished the last of the kibble yesterday. Carolina has brought out an extension cord and plugged it into her camera. Two days ago I watched the farmer plant his corn. He never once looked at my window, not even when I took off my shirt and pushed my breasts to the glass. I'm so horny I could cry. The Swedes have been playing "Werewolves of London" non-stop. With Remus dead, my time over, and Accalia watching from her car, I no longer know what anyone wants. The sun sets and Georg's Land Rover drives past Accalia's Fiesta. He returns an hour later. The music stops. Silence buzzes in my ears. I smell a new dog.

Georg drags an undocked Rottweiler behind him and locks him in the run. He then picks up the birdbath and throws it at my windows. It shatters against the steel bars. Shards of glass and crumbling concrete fly into my garret, but the bars hold. The scents of fresh manure, perfumed vampire, and virile Rottweiler fill my room. Georg floats up just beyond reach. "Is this new stud more to your liking?"

I say nothing and watch the twilight deepen in the cloudless sky. Moonrise looks to be about half an hour away.

The Rottweiler spins in circles and barks as he catches my scent. He's deep-chested with a full tail—strong and masculine in ways Remus had never been.

My knees start to bend. I grip the window sill.

Carolina picks up the camera.

Jon squeaks the rubber penis and rubs it between his legs.

Accalia's Fiesta idles on the road.

The Rottweiler's barking intensifies.

I force myself to keep my hindquarters down.

The cedar windbreak is starting to glow with a silver backlight.

Georg smiles and extends his palm to Carolina.

She rolls her eyes and stays with her camera.

Georg turns to me. "Fuck the dog."

I shake my head and try to refocus the Swedes. "What happened to Mary?"

Carolina glances at Georg but neither respond.

I move closer. Glass crunches under my feet.

Eventually Jon stops squeaking the rubber penis. "She couldn't handle the boredom."

"What's that got to do with anything?"

Carolina scowls.

Jon takes a deep breath. "Suicide."

I grip the bars. "Why do you stay in the Program, then?"

Georg bites his lip.

Carolina shakes her head. "*Det finns inget dåligt väder, bara dåliga kläder.* Everything we are doing is being viewed and judged. It is being like the hunting of witches again."

Jon glares at Georg. "We've allowed ourselves to become domesticated."

I roll my eyes. "When was the last time any of you tasted living blood?"

Carolina wrinkles her nose. "*Ingen aning.* We could be asking you the same thing."

I nod. "Yeah, I agree. We're all pathetic."

While we talk, the Rottweiler begins to chew at the chain-link. Metal bends.

On the road, Accalia continues to watch through her binoculars.

Carolina points to where the moon is rising. "*Se!* If you want to be going home, just be giving what we are wanting."

My lip curls. "I'm not fucking a dog."

"Why not?" Jon throws the rubber penis to the ground. "We've seen the messages on your phone. The Bernese Mountain Dog? The Irish Wolfhound? The Great Dane? You've done it before. Many times."

I clench the bars. During my estrus last year, a Bernese Mountain Dog had followed me to our den. When my dam saw him thrusting against my leg as I tried to hold him off, she called me a slut and I shifted. Unfortunately, the dog's owner organized an extensive search and his eventual discovery of the mutilated corpse outside our den meant we had to move. My dam said she had no pity for a depraved bitch who couldn't keep her hindquarters down and kicked me out of the pack before I could make a move on my sire or my littermates. Randall, Lowell, and my sire swore that would never happen and begged for leniency.

Eventually my dam agreed to the compromise of the Community Reintegration Program. I'd be able to come home only after I'd learned restraint.

Jon picks up the rubber penis and squeaks it again. "I know you want it."

My first placement in Parry Sound ended when a stray Irish Wolfhound somehow got onto the property and tried to hump me. I shifted and ripped him apart. Then, there was Brutus. I still don't know what turned him on. I release the bars and growl at Jon. "You didn't read the complete message threads. For an eternal creature, you have an amazing lack of patience."

"Enough of this tail chasing!" Georg opens the run. He scoops up the Rottweiler and floats up to my window. "It is time you met Mars."

The Rottweiler—Mars—barks.

I step away from the window.

Carolina floats up and points her camera into my garret. "You will be smiling now."

Mars smacks his lips.

I start to swoon.

Jon laughs and squeaks the rubber penis.

The sky brightens.

"Leave me alone!" I will not give in. No matter the full moon. No matter my estrus. No matter my stupid lupine body thinking a Rottweiler is an appropriate sexual partner. No matter these bored and grieving vampires toying with me or my whacked-out caseworker testing me beyond all reason. "I'm going home!"

Georg laughs.

As the moon rises over the cedars, I feel its pull. Strong. Tempting. I throw myself onto my cot and bury my face in the bare mattress.

Jon stops squeaking the rubber penis. "What are we going to do now?"

I keep my face in the mattress.

Georg clears his throat. "You will digitally stimulate the canine."

"Ew." Jon's voice floats farther away. "No way."

"Carolina?"

"*Nej!*"

"Then I will do it myself." Georg's voice comes closer.

Mars barks once more then begins to whimper. I keep my head down but can imagine him thrusting into the air as Georg manipulates him.

Carolina hisses. "*Din snuskhummer!*"

I smell prostatic fluid. I slip to the floor and pull the mattress on top of me. "Stop molesting Mars!"

"Then fuck him." Georg's voice is hard as stone.

I can't imagine my dam letting herself get caught in a situation like this. But she's not here to help me. And all Accalia does is watch through her binoculars. None of my caseworkers has ever told me how I'm supposed to resist anything. No tips, no suggestions, no twelve steps. This Program is so unfair. I should have been done days ago. At this rate, I'll never be allowed to go home. My rage runs cold. I throw off the mattress and get to my feet.

Carolina holds her camera steady.

Jon floats up and squeaks the rubber penis again.

Georg presses Mars to my window.

I take off my shirt.

Jon rubs his hands together.

Mars whimpers.

I roll down my shorts, untie my hair, and look Georg in the eye. "Is this what you want?"

He nods.

Slowly and deliberately I shake my head. "Never." I stand tall and look at the moon. I let my fur grow, my eye teeth lengthen, and my body distend. It feels good. Powerful. Calming. My claws go sharp.

•

Waning Gibbous (Sunday, April 5)

I wake naked in the cornfield, the rising sun warming me as crows pillage the newly-planted corn. The mingled scents of dirt, manure, and undead blood tinged with sandalwood, vanilla, and rose oil fill the air.

I get to my feet and jog back to Ruthven House. My window bars have been ripped from the wall and lie across the crumpled chain-link run. Tufts of red fur flutter in the breeze.

Still in shadow, Georg's corpse is impaled on the remains of the swing set, a wooden support beam piercing his chest and a net bag of garlic cloves stuffed in his mouth. Carolina and Jon's decapitated bodies have been jammed in the garbage bins. The ten-speed has been torn in half. As the sun's rays hit the Swedes' exposed skin, their corpses smoke and crumble to greasy ash. I pick up Carolina's camera and smash it against the brick wall of the House.

Mars is nowhere to be found, although his tracks lead me around the house before disappearing across the gravel road and into another cornfield. Accalia's silver Fiesta is in the driveway—upside down with the windshield punched in—lying on top of the Land Rover. Her body is still buckled in her seat, her throat slit with three parallel gashes, an unopened vial of wolfsbane clutched in her fist. I find dried blood under my fingernails.

I am so fucked. My dam will never forgive me. I reach into the Fiesta and grab Accalia's phone. I call home to apologize for failing the Community Reintegration Program—there's no way I'll get another transfer after this—but a recorded message says the number is no longer in use. I check Accalia's contacts and find my dam's new number, listed with an address in the Muskokas.

She answers on the third ring. "It's done?"

It's so good to hear her voice. I choke up and can't even get out a hello.

"Accalia?" My dam's voice turns sharp. "Is the little slut dead?"

I curl my lip. My mind works through the ramifications. My dam had never agreed to a compromise at all. Somehow, she must have seen my wakening sexuality as a threat to her dominance. That is so twisted. I grow cold again.

I power off the phone and pry the vial of wolfsbane from Accalia's fingers. Then, I go back into Ruthven House, get dressed, and stuff my things into my backpack. I slip the wolfsbane into my pocket then find the keys to the Jag in Mary's vault.

Greasy ash coats the Jag's front seat. I clean it off with my Bisclavret towel, throw my pack in the back, start the engine, and go see Mr. Talbot. I thank him for his friendship, exchange my remaining vouchers for fresh meat, and say good-bye. Then, I get on the county highway and head for the 401. I'm going home.

To Sift the Sacred
Brian Rappatta

*…life's long toil: to liberate the just from the convenient,
the mind's pure thought from the dredge of the
commonplace,
to sift the sacred from the profane…*

Jor paused in his work. Three corpses left. Just the perfect amount.

Such days were rare, and to Jor's mind, harbingers of good fortune, when he could leave off his day's labor in the thanatorium at an opportune point: the final arrangement of lines in a character, or the perfect combination of characters to form a word, or even rarer still the final positioning to finish a line. But never before had the bodies been just perfectly sufficient to finish character, phrase, line, and stanza all in one final flourish.

Jor felt a minor twinge of guilt. Was it wrong to be happy that the corpses had been so plentiful of late, especially when it evidenced the hardship of the commonfolk during the long days of winter? But he shrugged off the stab of conscience; his paean was for the glory of Scion; the boy-god was justified in calling as many souls to Him as he saw fit.

Three left. Jor considered them carefully, wondering in what order he might send them to their communion with Scion. One was an older man, more than twice Jor's age, with a hard-lined face and streaks of gray in what remained of his receded hair. His age was unusual. A lifelong bachelor, or perhaps an impotent, for him to have found his way so late in life to the preparing room of the boy-god's thanatorium. His clothes were shabby, and his fingertips frostbitten, so Jor surmised he must have been an indigent, to have died from exposure to the cold.

The other two were closer in age to the common acolytes of the boy-god. One, Jor guessed to be about five; judging by the boy's bony chest beneath his jerkin salvaged from bits of burlap bagcloth, he must have been a victim of malnourishment. All too common these days, especially in light of the poor harvests from the outlying farms. He was a prime candidate for the end of a stanza, with his head of golden curls and bright blue eyes that now stared lifelessly upward, as if anticipating his resting place so far above. Jor liked to finish lines and stanzas with boys such as this; their youth and innocence would be pleasing to Scion— fitting punctuation for a paean to the boy-god.

But Jor instead found himself gravitating to the third body. A boy, maybe twelve, who might once have been beautiful—it was difficult to say any longer. What remained intact of his face was matted with dried blood; the entire left side of his face caved in to a sickening tangle of dried gore. Jor had seen worse accidents, but this was likely no accident. More likely the boy had been murdered. Bludgeoned by the truncheons of the town guard for some slight offense, perhaps. Jor had long since learned to keep his emotions separate from his work, yet he could not hold back a sudden misting in his eyes as he imagined this boy's unfortunate end. A murder most profane, indeed.

So he decided to send the old man first, then the youngest boy. He stood over the tables where they'd been laid out for him. He crossed their arms across their chests to prepare them for their final sleep, then bent down over them and peeled open their eyes so they could spend their eternity contemplating the majesty of the heavens.

Then, he closed his own eyes, took a deep breath, and surrendered himself to the vibrations of the Interstices around him. The magic surged up inside him, filling his gut like a reassuring draught; his othersense came to the forefront of his consciousness. He ceased to see, but rather *felt* only the cold stone walls of the temple around him. He let his othersense diffuse even further, drifting upward, ever upward, up into the heavens, until he felt the unique vibrations of Scion's moon far above him.

He compensated for the moon's celestial path and found the exact spot where he had deposited the final body from last night's batch of deceased. He concentrated, and thrummed the vibration connecting his physical body with consciousness. It resonated like the singing of a harpstring. Then, he focused his magic, and opened a wedge in the space between the crest and the trough of the vibration. With the ease of long practice, he widened the wedge, creating an aperture in the space between existence, and then widened the aperture until it could accommodate a body. He wrapped the aperture around the old man, allowed it to close, sent it on its way all the way up the vibration, and opened the exit in the exact spot he'd chosen for this man's final resting place.

Jor triggered the stitch, and laid the man's body to rest on Scion's moon far above.

Then, he did the same for the other two bodies, arranging them in such a fashion that the angles of their bodies in their final repose formed the words of his paean. Together, these three completed the final rune of the final word of the stanza: *profane*.

When he was finished, he lingered for a few moments in the vibration, seeing only through the filter of the resonance the fruits of his handiwork. Three more bodies to join the community of the departed with the boy-god on the surface of His moon far, far above, where their bodies would never decay, and where they could stare forever at those they had left behind on this earth.

Jor envied them, in a way. So many times he'd been tempted to step through his own stitch to behold the surface of Scion's moon, but he knew he dared not. The boy-god's moon was only for those who had passed from their bodies to be with Him. The living could not walk on Scion's moon… none who had tried had ever returned.

"*Sermela m'shalan*," Jor muttered the traditional blessing for the acolytes of the boy-god. He hoped these three would find their rest, and that they would be pleased with being one small part of his paean in honor of his god—a paean that would forever be between himself, the god, and those dead who formed part of it. No one on this earth could ever hope to navigate the resonances in exactly the same fashion as he had to be able to read his words written in corpses.

"*Sermela m'shalan*, Jor-Cthnir," a woman's voice said softly.

Jor let the otherperception of the deep sensing fade and

opened his eyes. He was no longer alone. He turned, and saw an old woman clad in the traditional black hooded robe of the Aahd. Her hood was down, and the ghostly-white skin of her face seemed to glow in the meager torchlight from the temple's preparing room. Jor had spent time among the Aahd, and had learned to control his fear of their phantasmal features and violet eyes, yet he shuddered despite himself. "You startled me, abi," he said, according her the traditional greeting due an Aahd matron. Force of habit; had he considered the sacrilege of her presence, a non-believer in the temple of the boy-god, he might have scolded her instead.

"My apologies." She advanced into the torchlight, and he saw that she carried a cloth-wrapped bundle cradled in her arms. "I hoped not to disturb your magic."

Jor considered the bundle. "I am sorry for your baby, abi," he said. "Do you come to have me send it to lie on Scion's moon?" Such traditions were rare for the Aahd, who did very little honor to the bodies of their dead, preferring instead to bury them in the ground. But it was not unheard of for some of the Aahd to have adopted the traditions of their neighbors to the north.

"No," she said. "I came looking for you, Jor-Cthnir."

Jor frowned. "You must mistake me for someone else, abi," he said. "I am merely named Jor."

She shook her head. "I am not mistaken. You are the Jor who came with his master, Aramin, to live among us last summer. You were our honored guest."

Jor could not remember this woman from the summer he'd spent among the Aahd, but that was no surprise. Especially in high summer, the Aahd wore their hoods drawn and their robes tight around them to protect their colorless skin from the sun. He might have passed this woman dozens of times a day and never known her face.

"I am that Jor," he said. "And the fortune was mine. Yet the second syllable you give my name is in error. I have not yet fathered a child."

"You are mistaken," the woman said. "You knew my daughter, Aioi."

"Aioi…" he murmured. The name stirred a faint memory—of a smile rather than a complete face. He did remember, but only vaguely. One of the Aahd maidens, roughly his own age. She had been beautiful, hadn't she…? "I—"

The old woman smiled at his confusion. "I did not expect you to remember, boy. Your mind was addled by liver wine. Don't worry; you're not the first northerner not to know his limits with our drink. But my daughter remembered you, Jor-Cthnir. She carried your child."

Jor caught another fragment of a memory: a light kiss on the cheek as he slept off the first and worst hangover of his life…

He shook his head, and looked again at the bundle in the woman's arms.

"Aye," the woman said. She stepped a few paces closer and gently handed the bundle over to him, supporting the back of its head.

"I—" Jor accepted the bundle awkwardly. Had his initial assumption been incorrect? Was this baby alive? "Is he—?"

"He is dead," the old woman said.

"Oh." Jor had seen plenty of dead infants before, had sent hundreds to their rest on Scion's moon above, and included dozens more in the runes of his paean, yet as he peeled back the blanket to look at this one's face—his *son*—he swallowed a sudden painful lump in his throat.

"He is yours now," the old woman said. "As is our custom." Her voice caught in her throat.

He looked up from the baby in alarm. "Then—Aioi…"

"She did not survive the birth."

"I—I'm sorry, abi," Jor said.

She shrugged. "The fault is not yours, lad. You planted her with child, and she was proud to carry the son of a northerner. The fault was hers."

Jor wanted to argue that Aioi was merely the victim of ill luck, but he could find no words to refute the Aahd belief that women who died in childbirth were to blame for their own inadequacies. So instead he merely looked back down at the baby's face again.

"I think he has your eyes," the old woman said, and turned to leave.

She made it most of the way to the door before Jor could find voice to call after her. "Wait!" he said. "I—I can't send him to Scion's moon. He's—"

The woman turned back to regard him. "Do with him as you will, Jor-Cthnir," she said. "He is your son."

She left.

•

"I thought I might find you here."

Jor started guiltily at the voice. He instinctively crumpled up the parchment he held in his hands and turned to see who had disturbed him.

High Priest Ledsil, the administrative overseer of the entire Academy and its various collegiae, strode forth onto the balcony.

"Your Grace," Jor greeted Ledsil. Jor stirred guiltily, though in truth the balcony was meant for the use of all the novitiates, even at this late hour. It provided the best view anywhere in the Academy of the firmament. At the moment, Utierr, the father moon, was ripe, with Valasar not far behind, and Scion merely a thin silver sliver in the night sky.

"Father," Ledsil greeted Jor. Jor had been greeted with this honorific for the past two days, ever since he underwent the rite of conveyance to worship of Utierr, and it still rang false in his ears, as if it was meant for someone else. Hearing it from the lips of the high priest himself finally made it feel… permanent. Jor now owed his worship to Utierr, the father god.

Ledsil drew near enough to lay his hands on Jor's shoulders. "I regret not having been able to attend your conveyance ceremony, my boy," he said. "I would have liked to personally thank you for your service in the thanatorium."

Jor bowed his head. "You are too kind, Your Grace."

Ledsil smiled. "Not at all. You were quite difficult to replace."

"I… I am certain Eri will do an admirable job."

"Oh, I've no doubt Eri can get the souls of the poor departed up onto Scion's surface; I'm not worried about that. But he has little of your… zeal. And none of your gifts for words."

Jor failed to stifle a slight choke of surprise. "Your Grace?"

The high priest chuckled. "Oh, I know of your literary impulses, lad. And your talent. It was why I picked you out of the poets' college for the job in the thanatorium. I know all about your paean."

Jor stammered. "I—but how?" He knelt to the cold stone of the balcony. "Please, forgive me my presumption—"

"Do please stand up, lad," Ledsil said. "You have nothing to apologize for. I believe Scion would be quite honored by your unique form of worship."

"Then… have you read my paean?"

"Of course not. No farglass in my possession has the necessary precision to see with such detail onto the surface of Scion."

"Then… how did you know?"

Ledsil smiled slyly. "It is my business to know what happens in the thanatoriums. The worship of all the gods falls within my purview."

"I—of course."

Ledsil glanced down at the stone floor of the balcony, to the graveyard of crumpled parchments Jor had strewn about this night. "I take it the worship of Utierr does not fill you with such divine inspiration?"

Jor felt his face flush despite the chill of the midwinter night. "I am… still adjusting, Your Grace."

"Understandably so. As I recall, devotion to Utierr requires a certain shift in mindset. You would not be the first to struggle with the responsibilities fatherhood brings with it."

"I will adjust, Your Grace."

"I'm sure you will. Though it may not be necessary."

"Your Grace?"

"I understand your son only lived a matter of days. It may be the will of Scion that you continue to serve him. I could petition the bishops' assembly on your behalf to nullify your rites of conveyance to Utierr…"

Faint hope bloomed in Jor. Could he somehow manage to return to worship of Scion, so he could finish his paean?

But he squelched that hope. He bowed his head. "No, Your Grace. I do not wish that. Conveyance to Utierr means undertaking responsibility; I understood that part of my rites. I am a father now, even if I was only fortunate enough to be so for three days."

Ledsil accorded him a respectful nod. "Very well. I will abide by your wishes. Have you disposed of the infant's body, then?"

"I have. I—" Jor's voice wavered. "I buried him… privately." Which was a lie. In truth, the dead infant was still wadded in his blankets in a disused corner of the thanatorium; Jor hadn't been able to bring himself to bury him in a graveyard like his ancestors had done hundreds of years ago before they'd learned to harness the magic of the Interstices.

Ledsil grimaced. "I'm sure that must have been difficult for you, lad. It does the boy's spirit no honor to rot in the ground like a common unbeliever."

"He was half Aahd," Jor said. "Half unbeliever."

"You did not see fit to petition the bishopric to consecrate the boy's spirit to Scion?"

"It would not have made a difference," Jor said.

Ledsil conceded the point with a helpless gesture. The local bishop that oversaw the Academy and its various collegiae was notably inflexible in his demand for purity of the blood. "Well then," he said instead, "I suppose my only quandary then is what to do with you."

"Your Grace?"

The high priest indicated the wads of parchment littering the balcony. "The dean of the poets' college informs me you've become quite the drain on his stores of parchment."

"I—"

Ledsil held up a hand, and he smiled as if to assure Jor his words were in jest. He knelt down to pick up one of the crumpled sheets of parchment. Jor panicked, but thankfully the high priest did not uncrumple it to read the graveyard of unfinished runes on it. He merely held it up in his hand. "I imagine this must seem somewhat mundane, when until a few days ago your parchment was the firmament itself."

"I... yes, Your Grace." Jor did not add that the parchment felt completely unworthy of the gods.

"If I were a more selfish man, I would enlist your service among my own astronomers. We are making great strides in mapping out the firmament. Your talent for deep sensing would be put to good use."

Jor raised an eyebrow. He... an astronomer? At his age, he'd scarcely dreamed of such an honor. High Priest Ledsil had made no secret of his ambition to map out the firmament for as far as the deep sensing would allow, and boldly proclaimed it the divine will of the deictheon that the magic of the Interstices would one day enable them to set foot on other worlds in the firmament.

"But first I have a more pressing charge for you," the high priest said.

"Your Grace?"

"I need an emissary to the Aahd. Someone they already know, and trust."

Jor frowned. "But I don't understand. The treaty with them has already been negotiated. Are they not abiding by it?"

"This has nothing to do with treaty, lad. The Aahd have been quite conscientious about the shipments of grain. It's about respect."

"Respect? I'm not sure I understand."

"My most recent emissary seemed to think the Aahd were in dire need of converting to the worship of our deictheon. The Aahd… ahm… requested that he leave."

"Oh. I see."

"You fathered a son on an Aahd woman. As I understand it, that makes you one of them. We need that bond between our people and them right now."

Jor bowed. "I will endeavor to justify your trust, Your Grace."

"Spoken like a true poet, lad. You'll leave tomorrow."

•

Jor triggered the exit stitch and stepped out on Palauyäri, the northernmost island in the Ceriamaên archipelago. It was the island with the largest concentration of Aahd settlements clustered together around a central chieftain's dwelling. It was the nearest approximation of a government—and a capital—that existed among the Aahd.

In the only nine months of relations between their two peoples, the Aahd clanfolk had apparently grown accustomed to the sight of stitches opening in the midst of their settlements. The adults merely stopped what they were doing for a few seconds and turned their heads to see who had stepped out of the stitch materializing in the open air. The children, however, shouted with delight and flocked toward him.

"Abi Meirini said you would come back, Jor-Cthnir."

At thirteen, give or take, Ctvrin stood a head taller than most of the other children. He was the oldest of those children not yet "man-sharpened," as the Aahd referred to their ritual of passage. Jor realized the boy had readily addressed him in the Aahd fashion, in which parents adopted the first syllable of their firstborn son's name. It was a rather tacit gesture of acceptance, and Jor acknowledged it with a respectful nod.

Ctvrin looked puzzled at Jor's empty arms. "Where is your son? Have you not come to bury your infant?"

"I have already buried him. Privately." Jor shuddered at the memory of leaving his son to rot in the ground, where decay could claim his flesh and worms could feast on his eyeballs… it was not a fit sign of respect for the dead. "I came looking for Aioi instead."

Ctvrin frowned. "Did abi Meirini not tell you? She is dead. She died bearing your son."

"I know. I came to… I would like to see where she is buried."

"Why?"

Jor struggled to find the correct words. His command of the Aahd tongue was not sufficient for this task. "I wish to… pay respect."

Ctvrin giggled. "How can you buy respect from the dead?"

Jor frowned. Perhaps his translation hadn't been quite as accurate as he'd hoped. "It is… important to me. Please, can you show me?"

Ctvrin shrugged. He gestured for Jor to follow him, and set off across the settlement, past the tovi-hide huts of the matrons. He kept a brisk pace, beaming with pride at being Jor's guide, as those men and women they passed greeted Jor with something akin to the deference due a warrior returned from a hunt, all of them addressing him as Jor-Cthnir. Their welcome was warming; aside from the difficulties he had in resurrecting the words of their language in his memory to return their greetings, Jor felt as if he had never left. And indeed, once the Aahd welcomed you as clan, your welcome was permanent.

Ctvrin finally brought him to the burial plot about a half hour's march outside the settlement. It was little more than a grassless clearing among the banyan trees, devoid of any grave markings of any kind. The Aahd had no written language for such tasks, anyway.

"Where?" Jor asked.

"Here." Ctvrin gestured to indicate the entire clearing.

"No. I mean, where?" Jor pointed to the specific spot of ground beneath his feet. "Here?" He pointed to another spot of earth. "Or here? Where?"

Ctvrin frowned, not comprehending. But then his face lit up in recognition. "Will you unbury her with your magic?" He seemed eager to see a demonstration of Jor's Interstitial abilities.

"Ahm—no. I merely wish to… stand above her."

Ctvrin looked disappointed. But he considered for a moment, and then led Jor to a spot roughly in the center of the plot. "Here," he said. "I think."

It was as close as he would get. "Thank you," Jor told him. "Please, may I be alone for a few moments?"

Ctvrin nodded. "Will you be staying? You are welcome in my family's hut."

"Your invitation is most gracious. I… yes, I would like to stay. Please give your family my thanks."

Ctvrin smiled, pleased. "I will ready your sleep mat, then." He began to withdraw.

"Wait," Jor called.

"Yes, aba Jor-Cthnir?"

"I… do you remember? What was Aioi's death name?"

"She was Abatneseweiuyo."

Jor's command of the Aahd ceremonial dialect was rudimentary at best. He could have lived the remainder of his life with the Aahd and not quite gleaned enough of the nuances of meaning for it to make sense. "What does it mean?"

"'She who reaches further.'"

Jor frowned. "I don't understand."

Ctvrin mimed a reaching motion with his arms.

"I understand the words. But why that name? Why 'she who reaches further?'"

"She spoke often of going to live with you, in the northlands. She wanted to be the member of our clan to travel farther than anyone."

"Oh. I see. Thank you."

Ctvrin nodded, and left him alone.

•

Jor spent much of the next several days in the graveyard, sitting on the spot where Aioi had been buried. He deep-sensed the terrain below the ground's surface, and found half a dozen gaps in the earth large enough for bodies to lay in. One of them belonged to Aioi, though he knew not which. Without stitching the bodies up to look at them under the light of the sun, there was no way to tell. And although he longed to see again the face of the girl who had birthed his child—her face was blurred by poor memory and too much drink on the night they had lain together—he resisted the temptation to do so. He didn't want to remember her face half rotted off and crawling with maggots.

So instead he sat above those half-dozen bodies, allowing the sun to turn his face pink. Even here far south of Yatëa the winter weakened the sun's potency; had it been high summer, his skin would have burned to a crisp, but the weather remained mild enough that he only garnered a mild sunburn.

Ctvrin came to find him on the third day. "What's that?" he asked, pointing to the parchment and quill pen Jor held in his hands.

"It's for writing," Jor answered.

"For what?"

"For writing. I am composing an elegy. For Aioi.

Abatneseweiuyo."

"What is an el-uh-gee?" Ctvrin pronounced the word carefully, as if afraid he might break it.

"It's a poem. To honor the dead."

"Like a death name?"

Jor nodded. "A very long death name."

"And those?" Ctvrin indicated the paper, the pen, and the ink pot lying on the ground at Jor's side.

"These are to help me remember the words."

"Is your memory bad, Jor-Cthnir?"

"Not really." Jor smiled ironically. "I can remember these words well enough." He showed Ctvrin the blank parchment. He'd stared at it for hours, but words refused to come. Somehow, writing in the mundane medium of pen an ink was nothing, when he'd grown so accustomed to laying his runes with the bodies of the dead in Scion's realm.

Ctvrin gave him a pitying look, as if this was merely some other lunacy to which the northerners were prone.

•

Jor roused early the next day, even before the Aahd matrons were about their breakfast cookfires. The dawn found him in the glade, still staring at the piece of parchment. He'd considered dozens upon dozens of opening lines, only to abandon them all. How could he effectively write an elegy to a girl whose face he could barely remember? Among her people, Aioi had been "She who reached farther." She deserved better than a paltry elegy to a drunken one-night tumble.

So he picked up his parchment, pen, and ink, and headed

back to the village. He found Umai-imani-mai, one of the oldest matrons of the village, about her braiding. He marveled at how her gnarled hands could still manage the intricate work required for the Aahds' garments.

"Jor-Cthnir," she said, greeting him with a smile, looking over the top of her braiding, though her fingers never paused. "I was told you were back. It is good to see you again."

"Thank you, abi-mai. I—"

"You have a question."

Despite the warming sun overhead, Jor wished for one of the Aahd's robes to hide his blush. "You are wise, abi-mai. Can you tell me about Aioi?"

Umai-imani-mai chuckled. "Always gawking at the stars, that one."

"She was? I didn't know."

The old woman nodded. "Used to tell silly stories to her brothers and sisters about the people that lived there." She chuckled. "Her mother and father beat her so many times when she was young, but they never succeeded in beating the fancy out of her."

Jor considered. The literal Aahd word for star was "night-eye," because they believed that those their gods deemed had lived a worthy enough life were rewarded in their death by receiving a third eye in the firmament with which to watch over their people below. To his knowledge, the Aahd had no concept of how the heavens worked... no astronomy to speak of. Aioi's stubborn invention of stars as residences for far-away people must have been near heretical to the Aahd.

How tragic, that Aioi's fancy was far truer than her people's ancient belief. Jor opened his mouth to comment on this, but closed it.

"Thank you, abi-mai." Jor opened his ink, dipped his pen, and wrote notes about what Umai-imani-mai had told him on the parchment. So absorbed was he in making sure he got down all her words correctly that he didn't realize until he was finished that she was staring at him suspiciously, and at the paper where he formed the letters.

He met her gaze, and she narrowed her eyes. "Some of your sorcery?" she asked.

"Um—sort of," he said. "It is… a spell… to help me never to forget."

"Hmm." She shrugged, as if disappointed that the paper did not disappear into a crackling stitch.

Jor spent the better part of the day chatting with the Aahd villagers, collecting as many remembrances as he could about Aioi. Many of them had fond memories of the girl; more yet told him in great detail of the great rift that had existed between the girl and her parents, who neither understood nor encouraged her imagination. Perhaps the best phrasing he encountered was from a boy slightly younger than Ctvrin: "She thought somethings out of nothings easier than passing wind." Jor made sure to jot the phrase down verbatim.

She reached further, indeed.

The faintest glimmerings of a few lines of his elegy were beginning to take shape by the end of the day. Ctvrin returned from his tilling in the fields and found Jor in the family's hut, poring over his day's notes. "Are all you northerners so strange?" he asked.

Jor frowned. "What do you mean?"

"Do you always spend so much time talking about the dead?"

"I—I merely seek to remember her."

"Your remembrance is so… laborious. She has a death-name. She will be recalled in the katani-mai's history of our village."

"I meant no disrespect."

"Why do you ask so much about her?"

"I—she bore my child. Among my people, becoming a parent is sacred. It commends us to our next god. She changed my life."

"I see." Ctvrin grinned. "So she took your virginity."

•

Jor woke late the next day, after a long night of tossing and turning. He felt the area around his sleepmat for his notes, but the area was empty. Frantic, he scoured the entire hut, completely empty of Ctvrin's family at this hour. They were nowhere to be found.

He stumbled out of the hut without bothering to dress. The Aahd girls gaped at his shirtless body in the morning sunlight; given their lack of skin pigmentation, going half-naked in the sunlight was not something that their men or boys would ever do. Jor wasn't sure if he was committing a grave breach of decorum, but he didn't care.

He found Enami, Aioi's younger sister, who was helping to scrub the soup pots. It took a fair bit of gesticulation and stammering—the Aahd had no words for paper or notes—but eventually he made her understand what he was looking for. Enami nodded and pointed to the morning's cookfire.

Jor's heart sank. The telltale crumblings of ashen parchment lay in the base of the embers. Ctvrin had used them for kindling.

•

Ctvrin found him at sunup the next day in the burial ground, standing ankle-deep amid skull and skeletons. Ctvrin gasped.

Jor barely paused in his work. He stitched a stray leg bone that had become detached from its owner from untold years of rotting in the ground, arranging it as the final part of the rune to complete the latest word. "Go fetch your people," Jor told the boy. "I'm nearly finished. I have something to read to them."

Ctvrin couldn't have understood the word *read*, but for once he didn't ask Jor for clarification. Wide-eyed, he stumbled out of the glade, back toward the village.

The Aahd villagers began assembling maybe a half hour later. One by one they came to stand in a circle around the perimeter of the glade, their mouths hanging open in shock at the ghastly array of bones and bodies before them. Though perhaps due to Jor's grim set of determination, or the naked display of his magic as he arranged the last few runes, they remained quiet.

When he was finished, Jor stood at the center of the bodies and addressed the villagers. "People of the Aahd," he said, "this is the elegy I composed for Aioi, death-named Abatneseweiuyo." He gestured to indicate the arrangement of bodies at his feet. "Listen to my words."

He read the words as he'd lain them, pointing to each in its turn, beginning at the outermost edge of the glade and spiraling inward in an ever-tightening gyre. By the time he was halfway through, much of Aioi's family was sobbing. As he continued, his voice ringing clear and loud over the villagers' silence, more and more of the Aahd joined them, until he was forced to bring the final stanza to a crescendo to be heard over the cries of the village folk.

He stopped. Those that were not sobbing outright wiped tears from their eyes. Had they understood, though? Did they comprehend the limited range of his poetry in their language? Moreover, were they able to grasp that the arrangement of the bodies was the key to the entire sorcery, that they corresponded to words?

Slowly, Ctvrin took a few steps to stand before the villagers. He pointed to a splay of arm bones that was repeated over and over as a refrain throughout the entire elegy. "Abatneseweiuyo?" he said, his voice questioning.

Jor smiled. The boy had correctly read the sequence of runes. He *had* understood. "Abatneseweiuyo," Jor said. "Reach further."

Jor strode through the bones, keeping his eyes fixed on Aioi's parents. They wiped their eyes. The gazes of all the other Aahd villages were inscrutable. Jor's heart slammed in his ribcage. Would these people reproach him for his sacrilege? If they did, the alliance with the Aahd farmers could come to an end this very moment.

He didn't think so. The Aahd attached no sacredness to the remains of the dead. Their reverence for their ancestors was never focused on the ground, but rather on the sea of gleaming eyes in the sky.

He came to stand before Aioi's mother and father. He accorded them a bow of respect.

Aioi's mother spoke first. "You do our daughter a great honor with your sorcery. No one has ever had such an incredible death-name."

"I will teach you this sorcery," Jor said.

The woman looked dubiously at the array of corpses.

"I'll teach you the easy version," Jor added hastily. "With pen and ink."

The woman smiled, though the concepts of pen and ink could mean little to her. At least not yet.

"There's something I have to do first. It might take me a little while."

He turned and considered the pile of bodies. Then, he triggered the largest stitch he'd ever opened in his life. It crackled as an enormous fissure opened in the air and spread across the surface of the glade, swallowing the bodies. The villagers all gasped in delight and instinctively took several steps backward.

Jor left them. He fell into the otherperception of deep sensing and sent his consciousness upward, faster and farther than he'd ever had cause to do so before. He sensed Scion's moon, and Utierr's, and even Valasar's in the landscape of his perception, but he did not stop there. He kept going, thrusting his consciousness out into the great emptiness of the firmament.

It might take him a while, but he'd find another moon, a resting place for these Aahd, where the eyes of their ancestors could watch over them, a place where they would rot no more.

Witching
Erin Kirsh

Hidden under the bed, a bucket of salt
water, carnelian nestled there like goldfish
shimmering in the depths, tiger eye flashes
in the dark. Cloudy cleansing water
pulls cursed words, stale divinations
from the stones. When the moon
takes center stage, Wife tucks curtains
into holsters softly like pushing hair
behind her ears. Husband
pools drool on the pillow next to her.
Wife bears the bucket to repose in rectangles
of moonlight patching the floor, lets it rest
in the beams like a cat, nocturnal. Wife won't sleep
while crystals spa, it is time
that teases her mind awake, the precise order
of events, how she will have to return
the stones to their fugitive home
beneath the bed before Husband wakes up
fresh lectures souring his breath. Wife purses her lips
considers how she'll attend to each drop
of spilled water on the floor

Erin Kirsh

to avoid suspicion, sweep salt circles
silent into dustbins. When Husband rises
in the morning, a regressed Apollo, his socked foot will meet
a solitary droplet, he will call the landlord
full of fury, imagining nothing less mundane
than a leak.

Star Trip(tych)

M.X. Kelly

1.

At the bottom of a snowy
mountain, looking up:
A moonlit sky and
stars sledding down.

2.

On the top of a hill:
A crystal panorama. A net
of diamonds spread out
over a midnight sea.

3.

In the skyscraper cities: nothing
but darkness. We dragged the stars
down to earth; our nights now veiled
in a grieving black mantilla.

Arcane History: An Interview with Fantasy Author Scott Thrower

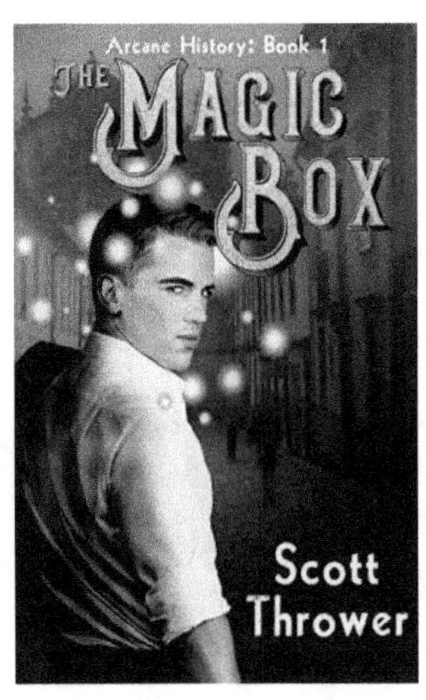

DFS: Before we talk specifics, could you give a log-line or elevator pitch for *The Magic Box?*

ST: *The Magic Box* is book one in the *Arcane History* series, about an university researcher who accidentally discovers that magic is real and releases it into 1915 Toronto.

DFS: What makes your work different? There's a lot of fantasy out there—what is unique about yours?

ST: I took some deliberate steps to make sure *The Magic Box* stood out in the world of urban fantasy (or, more precisely, gaslamp fantasy). I wanted Canadian representation rather than landing in one of the more marketable cities, and I wanted to explore the history of what Toronto was like at the time, from the smells of an industrialized city still chock full of horses, the tensions that came from war and growing population density, and the lonely, dangerous way of life forced upon gay men by social mores. But with magic.

DFS: What were you hoping to accomplish with your world-building, and what sources did you draw on?
ST: Writing historical fantasy can be dangerous because it easily leads to research paralysis. Setting it in the real world meant I had an obligation to get certain elements right. I spent a very long time reading about the state of medicine, transportation, and the early days of Toronto landmarks. The history of homosexuality in the city isn't well documented for obvious reasons, but I found some great transcripts from The ArQuives, a repository for gay history. One transcript even revealed that Toronto in the '10s and '20s had not just one but two gay mayors, though it wasn't commonly known at the time. Even so, most of The ArQuives material starts in the '60s and '70s. I even went on a disappointing walking tour about the city's cruising history and the Morality Department of the Toronto Police. Writing this book changed the way I walk around.

DFS: Disappointing how? Did your research change your perception or experience of the city?
ST: The tour descended into some vague history of the era rather than Toronto specifics, and my research had already gone deeper. The Morality Department was better funded than even the murder squad, and it was largely devoted to returning runaway wives and finding ways to catch gay men. It was a time when crowded homes and social mores made it impossible to bring home a date, so parks, alleys, and public bathrooms saw their fair share of use. The city reacted by redesigning parks in a hostile way

to minimize so-called unsavory use, and they even designed public washrooms so a policeman could lean a ladder against the outside wall and peek into the individual stalls to make sure you weren't doing anything too interesting. Depending on the soundtrack you put over it, it could be tragic or farcical. I mean, well into the century, a Toronto gay bar had a police booth inside so that patrons could be monitored and arrested as needed, later to have their names printed in the newspaper to ruin their lives. There's a lot that walking tour skimmed right over.

DFS: The ironically named "Morality Department" is a stain on the city's history. I'd say that we've progressed since then, but not enough. I think institutionalized bigotry and discrimination, at one time formalized by Toronto's police in the "Morality Department", can plausibly be connected to modern events: the alleged* police mishandling of the Bruce McArthur case is one example; Pride Toronto's decision to ban uniformed police from marching in the parade is another. To what extent do you think a historical understanding of institutions of discrimination is useful for understanding and discussing these kind of modern events? Do you think *The Magic Box* can play a productive role in that process towards better understanding?

***"alleged" added for legal reasons**

ST: I don't want to overstate the role of LGBTQ+ history in the book. It's an element I work with as much as I do the history of diabetes, since my main character suffers from that. But I think knowing how history played out gives much-needed context to the world today. The Black Lives Matter protest at the Pride Parade a few years ago brought up a lot of anger from people who didn't appreciate the parade being interrupted, but within the context of a very long history of poor treatment by police, it made sense. When people spend generations seeing the police as a source of fear, in many cases right up to present day, asking them to suddenly change their mind is unreasonable, especially when police reforms are still very much needed.

DFS: What influenced your decision to set your story in historical times rather than contemporary? Why did you settle on the era that you did?
ST: I knew I wanted to set the story in Toronto, because genre fiction overlooks Canada. I've always been in love with the past, and 1915 gave me a great intersectional point of wartime Canada, the massive societal change that was going on, and still being a few years before the invention of insulin. Having a character so close to death from a disease that could only be treated with starvation, and only temporarily, gave me a compelling starting point.

DFS: Let's talk about magic systems. How is magic handled in your books? How does it work?
ST: I have more than one magic system in play, and since the book focuses on the release of magic back into the world, the characters are forced to figure out how everything works through the course of the story. Unfortunately, that makes discussing the logistics somewhat of a spoiler!

DFS: I think the nature of Charlie's illness is another interesting and distinctive feature of *The Magic Box*. Can you talk about your narrative process as it concerns Charlie's disease?

ST: Charlie's diabetic, which was a death sentence before the invention of insulin. There were a number of attempted treatments, ranging from narcotics to carbohydrate training, but starvation was also high on the list. Medical photos of the era tend to show two things. The first is people so skeletally thin that you just want to look away, and the second is beds full of comatose patients who were never going to wake up. And the heartbreaking thing is starvation often worked—for short periods of time. There are stories about children treated through this method at the time who became so desperate for food that they were sneaking seed out of a bird's cage, and, of course, starvation is a death sentence in and of itself. But the idea of someone starving themselves knowing that it isn't a cure, that it's just a postponement of what at that time was inevitable, it really helps define a character for me. Charlie became someone who had an incredible amount of willpower because he was fighting for every last second—and he's fighting for Henry. Theirs is not a perfect relationship. It was a difficult time to be a gay man, particularly a poor one, but there's something between them that keeps Charlie fighting for every moment he can get.

DFS: How would you categorize your introduction of the magic—a portal fantasy, like *Alice in Wonderland*, where an ordinary character is brought into a magic world; an intrusion fantasy, like *Dracula*, magic intrudes into the ordinary world of the character; or an immersion fantasy, like *Lord of the Rings*, the characters live in a magic "secondary world". What category best fits *The Magic Box*, and why did you take that narrative strategy?

ST: *The Magic Box* is very much an intrusion fantasy. I'm trying to set up Toronto as it was at the time, warts and all, and since magic is then added to the equation through the course of the story, part of the fun is seeing how that spins out and affects history. In 1915, the British Empire was very much embroiled in World War 1, so having access to magic almost parallels the changing face of war and the technological revolution going on at the time. Science changed the way we fight, even taking it up into the air. I like the idea of magic in terms of an arms race, which takes a simple idea of cantrips up to a huge scale so quickly. The stakes are amazing.

DFS: Some critics distinguish "hard fantasy" and "soft fantasy" based on the emphasis placed on rules and limitations in magic systems. Brandon Sanderson says that resolving conflicts with magic is only satisfying to the extent that the reader understands the rules of the magic. Can you talk a bit about your thoughts on these issues in relation to the magic systems of your stories?

ST: Magic is a tricky thing to play with as a writer, just as science can be. We've all seen episodes of *Doctor Who* where the sonic screwdriver suddenly has a new ability that just happens to show up at the right time, and it's not a satisfying feeling as the credits roll. But sometimes the story isn't about that hurdle and the sonic is just a shortcut to get us to the emotional crux of the story. Ideally the two work together—the logistical conclusion and the emotional one—but sometimes you have to skip the head and just play to the heart.

DFS: There's been a call for greater diversity in the fantasy genre. How do you see your writing in this broader discussion?

ST: I grew up gay in the 80s, hunting for any scrap of gay content in late movies in CityTV, so I knew when I started writing that I wanted to show the characters that I so desperately needed to see when I was a kid. There's a lot of value in seeing yourself in the media you breathe in without those characters being neutered sidekicks or, as so often happened in early gay representations, as the perverted villain. LGBTQ+ characters remain underrepresented in genre fiction except, all too often, as objects designed to titillate, so I try to focus on realistic characters rather than hypersexualizing. I'm also trying to push back on the idea that just because my main character happens to be gay, I've written a gay book that only gay people will be interested to read. (Or, more likely, heterosexual women, who make up most of the readership of gay novels at the moment.)

DFS: What do you think about the #ownvoices movement?
ST: I see value in the #ownvoices movement. Particularly among self-published authors, most gay fantasy is written with romantic or erotic overtones by women, which can be frustrating when I'm looking for a feeling of authenticity—even with wizards and werewolves involved. I think every writer can write outside of their experience, providing they put in the necessary work to understand what they're doing, but not everyone is self-aware enough to know when they've stepped into harmful caricature or are otherwise just missing the mark.

DFS: What do you think of the tendency in romance novels to depict relationships at their inception—focusing on the will they/ won't they tension—rather than focusing on the struggles of sustaining a relationship?
ST: Writing a relationship from the beginning makes sense for dramatic tension. The emotions are much more fraught in those will they/won't they contexts, and readers get excited to feel those moments again, however vicarious. I jumped into the middle of

the relationship instead, already having my couple shacked up, but that's because I was more interested in the era and how difficult it would be to maintain a long-term gay relationship in a closeted society, particularly given how hard it would be to find compatibility when your dating pool is limited to the men you've met in a park at night while trying to dodge the police. I liken it to queer dating in a small town now. You have to make concessions, and you have to work harder at making things work because you're not exactly spoilt for choice.

DFS: How do you strike a balance between the fantasy and romance elements of your novel? How did you decide which of the two genres to emphasize?

ST: It's not a traditional romance, since we're starting in the middle of the relationship and stumbling on from there. Charles is a very focused character, an intellectual who tends to lose track of things when he has a goal, and the series doesn't shy away from the fallout of such single-mindedness. I wanted to focus primarily on the story and the world, and the relationship is collateral.

DFS: Contrary to some literary critics who think speculative fiction is less serious than realist fiction, I think fantasy and science fiction often explores important themes and concepts— better than realist literature in some cases. Can you talk about how you've used speculative elements and the fantasy genre to explore issues of importance to the human experience?

ST: I think that we are emotional creatures, and we don't just shut that part of ourselves off when we decide to pick up a fantasy novel or listen to a fairy tale. We bring our whole selves into the act of reading. I actually think speculative writing has an advantage in reaching the profound, which the original *Star Trek* series demonstrated so beautifully. Sometimes they were just hitting a rubber suit with a rock, but they were also confronting difficult topics that people weren't able to talk about, especially on network TV. That's so much harder now due to the end of monoculture in media. We're now siloing ourselves so that we're only confronted with what we want to see. *The Magic Box* asks some big questions in a similar way once you look past the jolly good adventure, but the presence of magic in no way invalidates any points the story's making about discrimination, responsibility, or egotism.

DFS: Have you had any unexpected reactions to your stories, or any feedback that has really stood out or affected you? Do you like hearing from and communicating with readers, and is there a good way for fans to connect with you?

ST: I have a long history of interacting with my readers and podcast listeners, and I've found it very rewarding and, alternately, heartbreaking. I believe that once my work is out of my hands, I have no control over it. No two people will get the same thing out of a story. The podcast has been out longer, so I've had much more feedback for that, but it has ranged from people who have decided to try writing for themselves to others who have taken strength from it in difficult circumstances. There are also others who've listened to my voice for so long that they feel safe reaching out in moments of crisis, and you have to draw that line very clearly as you direct them to proper resources. That said, the podcast has a discussion group on Facebook where I remain a very active member, and I'm always on Twitter with the handle @periodicallypod.

image credit: Brian C.E. Baker

Scott Thrower is an award-winning playwright and the creator and writer of the *Fairy Tales for Unwanted Children* podcast and its associated published works. His first novel is called *The Magic Box*, one of three released books in the *Arcane History* series.

Craft: Writing Thoughts in Third Person

How should you write a POV character's thoughts when using a third-person narrator? Ultimately it's a matter of subjective taste and the needs of the particular story you're writing. Still, it's worth considering the dimensions of this kind of craft decision.

First, let's consider the types of third person narrator. The biggest three are third-person omniscient (third omni), third-person limited (third limited), and third-person cinematic (cinematic). In third omni, the narrator can move freely into the minds of multiple characters, giving us their inner thoughts. In third limited, the narrator tracks a single POV character, and is only able to narrate that which the POV character would know, think, or perceive. In cinematic, the narrator is like a floating camera that can describe the action, but can't enter the mind of any character.

Cinematic loses one of the greatest strengths of prose fiction, which is the ability to render the inner mind of a character and give us a window into someone else's experience. Third omni is somewhat out of style, though it was used to great effect by writers like Tolkien who, for example, briefly delved into the mind of a rabbit as it wondered what a pack of hobbits was doing so far out of their usual territory. Effective third omni requires a strong authorial voice; it is also challenging to effectively guide the reader's mind without giving them whiplash from jumping between characters. Third omni is an effective viewpoint when used well, but it is hard to pull off. Third limited seems to be the default nowadays (along with first person). I would guess that it is what most readers are expecting, and by using it, you aren't going to raise any eyebrows.

Whether we're writing in third omni or third limited, we still need to modulate how close we are to the minds of the characters we are narrating. This aspect of prose craft is called "psychic distance". Consider the following paragraph, which moves through several levels of psychic distance:

There was a pie on the windowsill. Billy was hungry. I'm going for it, Billy thought. Yum! Blueberry!

This passage moves from objective statements outside of the character's head ("There was a pie on the windowsill"), to narrative reports/summaries of a character's mental state ("Billy was hungry"), to transcriptions of direct thought mediated by the narrator ("I'm going for it, Billy thought"), to stream of consciousness unmediated by the narrator ("Yum! Blueberry!").

As we approach the mind of the viewpoint character, writers sometimes feel the need to indicate, through language or typography, that a thought is being presented. Consider the following four formulations:

1. I'm going for it.

2. *I'm going for it.*

3. I'm going for it, Billy thought.

4. *I'm going for it*, Billy thought.

In the first variation, there are no added markers, and the reader is expected to infer that the sentence is Billy's thought. In the second variation, italics typographically signal a thought. In the third variation, the verb "thought" linguistically signals a thought. In the fourth variation, both language and typography are used to signal a thought. These are the basic strategies for marking thoughts.

Tastes differ, but I have a strong preference for the first strategy, which is also called "free indirect discourse"—narration that slips freely in and out of the mind of the POV character. Jane Austen used the style consistently and popularized it in the British novel. The style spread widely, and was used by authors such as Flaubert, Hemingway, Woolf, Joyce, and Kafka. The style is also called "deep POV".

The fourth variation ("*I'm going for it*, Billy thought") feels like too much hand-holding for my taste, and draws attention to itself. I would say that picking either the second or third strategy is preferable to combining them; either of them do the trick, so using both introduces unnecessary redundancy.

The third variation ("I'm going for it, Billy thought") uses a verb to attribute the thought to Billy. This is a good method, but it's important to recognize that it is distancing the reader from Billy's mind; the presence of the words "Billy thought" means that this statement belongs to the narrator, not Billy, putting the reader at a slight remove from Billy's mind. That's not necessarily a bad thing, but it's a dimension of craft that's worth considering when deciding how to render thought. If you want your narration to feel more inside of your POV character's head, then you will generally want to avoid "thought" attributions. Moreover, "thought" verbs, much like perception verbs—words like "saw", "heard", "watched"—are weak; they don't add any colour to the mental image, and they introduce a distancing filter between the reader and the POV character. It's worth noting that using thought verbs is consistent with free indirect, because you can still mix direct thoughts in with the narration; however, if you are using italics for direct thoughts, then your POV character can never fully take control of the narrative (there will always be, at the very least, a typographical fence). For that reason, I prefer using "thought" verbs over italics.

The second variation ("*I'm going for it*") uses italics to typographically mark the sentence as a thought. The sentence belongs to Billy, not the narrator—we are inside Billy's head at this point—and the italics signal that shift to the reader. This kind of typographical marking serves primarily to avoid confusion—to make sure the reader knows when the shift is happening and when it is over. In this way, the typography builds a kind of fence around thoughts. Italics are a guide for the reader, and it is probably for this reason that italicized thoughts are more common in YA. There are two big reasons why I prefer to avoid typographical markers (most commonly italics) for thoughts. By fencing in thoughts, we implicitly say that everything outside of the italics is outside of the POV character's head, which makes the overall narrative feel more removed from the character's experience. By contrast, in the absence of typographical fences, there is a bleed-over of the character's mentality into the narration (an effect achieved through free indirect discourse or "deep POV"). Secondly, there may be times when you will want the reader to take a moment to figure out to whom the sentence belongs, or times when you will want to create a genuine ambiguity. This technique is only available to you if you are not relying on typographical indicators, so in that sense, the use of italics for marking thoughts reduces your power to achieve certain literary effects. (There is another benefit to avoiding italics for thought: you may want to use italics for other purposes; this could include writing the contents of a letter, for example, or as a typographical marker for psychic communication).

This leaves us with the final option: free indirect discourse. In this strategy, the narrator jumps freely in and out of the POV character's mind, mixing direct thoughts (unattributed and unmarked by typography) with regular narration. The reader is expected to tell the difference as they go. Naturally, writing in free indirect style requires care in crafting sentences so as to avoid causing confusion (in much the same way that it is difficult to write clear dialogue without using quotation marks). Luckily, there is a simple and effective trick for signaling thoughts: for past-tense narrators, a present-tense verb in a sentence will automatically signal a switch to the POV character. In the sentence "I'm going for it", the verb "to be" in its present tense form "am" signals that we have jumped into the POV character's mind; so too, for that matter, does the pronoun "I"—neither of these words could have been used by our narrator (third person, past tense), so they must be attributed to our POV character. In this way, directly presented thoughts can implicitly signal that they belong to the POV character, eliminating the need for thought attributions or typographical markers.

There is an important note for free indirect discourse: rarely do our thoughts conform to proper sentence structure—if our mental experiences are even linguistic structures at all—so to write free indirect effectively means accepting grammatically improper prose. If you write in this style, be prepared to use fragments, omit the subject (especially the first-person pronoun), shift tenses, and generally break rules with some regularity. So, for example, to convert "He thought the pie smelled delicious" to free indirect, we wouldn't simply change the pronoun and tense to "I think the pie smells delicious", which is stilted and awkward; instead, we would reformulate the words to better reflect interiority, something like "Mmm! Fresh blueberry—smells like mom used to make!"

A writer doesn't need to rely solely on one strategy or the other. In free indirect discourse, "thought" verbs can be used to ease the transition from objective narration to stream of consciousness by providing an intermediary level of psychic distance. It's possible to shift strategies even within the space of a sentence; one clause could belong to a deep pov character, and another clause in the same sentence could belong to our third person narrator (however, typographical choices, like italics, should remain consistent). It is often advantageous to zoom in or out of the POV character's mind. A moment of deep introspection or a moment of heightened emotional intensity may call for a deeper focus on the POV character's mind; in sudden shifts to stream of consciousness, it is almost as though the POV character, overwhelmed by the situation, grabs control of the narrative from the third-person narrator. That's just one example of an effect that can be created through control of psychic distance. A writer who is attentive to psychic distance can craft sentences to achieve the intended "zooming" effect.

My preference for internal thoughts in third person is free indirect discourse. Of course, it depends on subjective tastes and the needs of your story, but I think that writing thoughts without any typographical or linguistic markers—combined with a third-person limited past-tense narrator—is an effective and reliable strategy that can safely be used by default, unless you have a good reason for doing otherwise.

Response 1: Brandon Butler

I've become a believer in setting my story in either first-person or third-person limited. That said, from time to time I will do a version of third-person limited where I never explicitly enter the thoughts of the POV character as a stand-in for dialog as in all four of the examples with Billy—although the relevant thoughts can be surmised by character descriptions and third-person summaries of a character's musings (i.e.: "Billy had thought about the problem all day, and had come to the conclusion that…").

But my rules are my own, and not for everyone. I have and

will continue to break them myself for what I consider the good of the story.

If I do decide my narrative will explicitly portray character thoughts in the manner of dialog, I will almost always make sure this feature is introduced early, preferably on the first page, accompanied by the general "Billy thought" attribution (or "thought Billy" if I'm feeling extra artsy). I do this to make it clear to the reader that these sorts of thoughts will be part of the narrative going forward. From that point on I will favor adding all other thoughts without attribution, only including them if they seem necessary either for sentence rhythm or clarity.

Part of the reason I do this is my own personal extension of George R. R. Martin's thoughts on the third person limited view: this is the way we generally experience the world, and fiction is best told through that lens. In that spirit, it's my own theory that rarely do real people think in actual sentences—perhaps they do when writing, but otherwise in my experience it's quite rare—and so it makes sense to try to tell a story where thoughts are not expressed that way. Rather, I find it better if you can find a way to surmise thoughts onto the character *by the reader.*

Real life does not make things so clear, so why should my story? Certainly, if it's a question of understanding what is literally going on or a character's motivations become incomprehensible, it should be time to express a character's thoughts—although this could also be accomplished through regular dialog. For me it's more fun for the reader to have a range of possibilities for the motives of a given character; it only requires that the character's actions are themselves plausible given their situation and who they are.

Which isn't to say I don't write many, many stories with direct thoughts. They can be a lot of fun.

So, to sum up, do what feels best to you. Character thoughts can be the most interesting parts of the story, and—whether told directly or not—they might even be where the real story happens. So let your imagination fly!

—Brandon Butler

Brandon Butler is a Nova Scotian author currently living in Toronto. He is a former winner of the *Writers of the Future* contest, and his work is forthcoming from or has appeared in *Selene Quarterly Magazine*, *Third Flatiron Publishing* and *Bad Dream Entertainment*.

Response 2: Y.M. Pang

I'm going to whole-heartedly... disagree. Sure, if you open up a book and it's littered with italicized thoughts, that could be off-putting. But the solution isn't to reformat the italics and call it a day. At that point, the writer might want to consider if they simply overused direct thoughts—and no amount of italic-banning is going to correct that.

The use of italicized thought is so common that readers instinctively know what it indicates, and would not feel particularly "distanced" because of it. How close the limited third-person POV is to the character is achieved by the diction, sentence structure, and uniqueness of the narration. It's not achieved by the presence or absence of italics around direct thoughts. If the overall narrative feels too removed, that's the fault of the narrative, not the fault of typographical choices for direct thoughts.

And at the end of the day, direct thoughts in a third-person narrative *are* shifts. There's no way around it, and the writer isn't going to achieve bleed-over purely by avoiding typography. Direct thoughts are a shift in POV, and more than likely a shift in tense too, because third-person present-tense stories aren't exactly common. Since it is a shift—and there's no way around it—why not mark it down with typography such as italics? Why not indicate to your readers: hey I know this is a shift, I know it's jarring, but it's intentional—I promise. If the marking isn't there, the reader—and editor—might file it away as a mistake.

Now, granted, I don't think any reader or editor would drop a book based on the presence or absence of italics for direct thoughts. So this probably isn't a point worth belabouring—as long as the story is consistent...which is why I really, really advise against shifting strategies within a single story (let alone a single sentence). Sure, "he/she/they thought" tags can be present at times and not present in others. But it's a bad idea to use italics for some direct thoughts and not for others. Remember what I said about the reader and editor filing away your choices as mistakes? That's going to happen doubly if you sometimes use italics and sometimes don't. Unless it's done in some kind of clear, consistent, pointed manner (e.g. there are two POV characters and one of them always uses italics for thoughts and the other always doesn't, and that signals something about their psyches), it's going to look like a mistake and a copyediting error. Why create this extra annoyance for your readers when you can ease them better into your story by being consistent, and allow them to focus on the plot twists, the characters, the worldbuilding... also known as, the things that actually matter?

There is one exception to all of this, one type of story where not italicizing direct thoughts would be advisable and even inconsistent italicizing could be considered. And that is a surrealist, stream of consciousness story. A story where the style and prose *want* to draw attention to themselves rather than simply providing a clear window to the narrative. If that's the story you're crafting, go for whatever typography is appropriate in the moment for direct thoughts—and the rest of your story, for that matter. But that type of narrative is so defiant to craft conventions in general that I scarcely see the point of mentioning it in an article on craft.

I agree the "he thought" "she thought" tags are unnecessary in third-person limited POV, since there should only be one person whose thoughts you can access at all in the given scene. "Thought" is almost as invisible as "said" though, so I can't see it causing a problem for most (or any) readers. The tags might be useful in an audio release to distinguish thoughts from speech, though the context, other characters' reactions, and the audiobook narrator's tone should probably render the tags unnecessary. (Basically, as long as the audiobook narrator does a good job, it'll be fine).

On the subject of direct thoughts, using David's phrasing, I'm going to say: "It depends on the needs of your story, but marking down direct thoughts with italics during third-person limited narratives is a safe strategy to use by default, unless you have a good reason for doing otherwise."

If you want an actual seamless way of conveying thoughts, direct thoughts just aren't the way to go, with or without typographical/linguistic markers. Indirect thoughts generally weave into the narrative better, since they convey the same information without a jarring transition in POV or tense. Compare (I purposefully used no typographical/linguistic markers as per David's "default" recommendation):

Mark stormed out of the classroom. I hate teamwork, especially with a bunch of idiots who always miss the deadline.

Mark stormed out of the classroom. He hated teamwork, especially with a bunch of idiots who always missed the deadline.

This works even better if the indirect thoughts are integrated into actions. The character's thoughts still become clear, but due to a combination of context and implication, not pure statement alone. Example:

Mark stormed out of the classroom. As he wrenched the door open, he shot a glare back at his group mates. They'd submitted their sections late on the last assignment, and if they dared do it again...

Now, if we were to take David's example, I'd write it as:

A pie sat on the windowsill. Billy's stomach rumbled, and he leaned forward. He bit down, filling his mouth with the taste of blueberry.

There are times when you *want* the jarring transition to first person, when you want to convey the character's exact thoughts, when you want the segment to stand out. But for mundane thoughts—like hating a group assignment or wanting a blueberry pie—there's no need to "tell" the thought when it can be easily shown. After all, the exact phrasing of the thought is really quite boring. And in those instances when you choose to use direct thought because you *want* it to stand out? Then why not use italics or linguistic markers? Why even pretend it's "integrated" into the text when it's clearly not, and not meant to be?

I think it's more fruitful to shift the conversation away from "what kind of typography should we use/not use in direct thought"—because at the end of the day, none of it matters. It's a shift in POV and tense, and it's going to jump out either way, with or without italics. Instead, I encourage writers to ask if all those direct thoughts really need to be there. With proper description, word choice, and good old show-don't-tell, you might find those direct thoughts didn't need to be in so many places to begin with.

—Y.M. Pang

Y.M. Pang is a Toronto-based author whose fiction has appeared in *The Magazine of Fantasy & Science Fiction*, *Strange Horizons*, *Clarkesworld*, and many other venues. She is a Submissions Editor with *Speculative North*, and a dabbler in photography and art.

Exercise: After the Battle

In prose fiction "psychic distance" is how close the narrator is to the mind of the viewpoint character. The purpose of this exercise is to practice with different levels of psychic distance while using a third person narrator. The point is not to suggest that any method is "best", but rather to isolate different techniques and pay close attention to their strengths and weaknesses. Every writing technique is a tool in the writer's toolbox, and familiarity with the tools enables writers to choose the best one for the job.

The idea of "Thoughts After the Battle" is to write a scene that takes place after a battle, while deliberately restricting psychic distance in a series of passages.

General requirements:
- Use a third-person narrator, with a single POV character
- Write a scene that takes place after a battle, in a speculative fiction setting
- Show, don't tell, the characters relation to the battle

Part A has three separate tasks (5 min each):
1. Write 1-2 paragraphs using only cinematic/objective POV. (Cinematic/objective is only details about the scene that would be available to observers. For example, "ashes blew across the field". No character thoughts/feelings are

allowed in this mode, except to the extent that they would be visible to an observer, such as a furrowed brow. You can use any sensory details or scene descriptions you like, but the POV is essentially a "camera" floating outside of the character's head with no access to their thoughts or feelings)

2. Write 1-2 paras using only thoughts and feelings mediated by the narrator.

   (Narrator mediation uses "thought" or "felt" verbs to describe what the character is going through. For example, "Standing over the bodies, Egar couldn't help but feel [...]", or "so much pointless loss, Egar thought").

3. Write 1-2 paras using only stream of consciousness from the POV character, without narrator mediation.

   (Stream of consciousness does not use "thought" or "felt" verbs from the narrator; it directly presents the POV character's unmediated thoughts. For example, "What senseless tragedy! There must be some survivors. A purple robe—Is that... Prince Cedric!")

Part B has only one task (5 min):

Compose 1-2 paragraphs by selecting and rearranging sentences from previous exercises. (Adding a word here-or-there as necessary). Make it as good as you can, without substantially changing anything.

The purpose of part A is to practice using different techniques by isolating them and using them exclusively. This forces us to deal with the limitations of that technique, and to find creative solutions.

The purpose of part B is to compare and contrast strengths and weaknesses of the different techniques, and to explore how those different techniques can be combined into a more compelling composition.

Two speculative fiction writers, Melissa Terry and Andy Dibble, have provided their takes on Part B of the exercise for illustrative purposes.

Exercise Example 1, by Melissa Terry

Carnage surrounded Kell. His brother lay in a heap at his feet, blood trickling from his mouth and seeping into the blue sand, turning it a deep purple. Kell would have done anything if only he could take his brother's place. Mehdi was the better man, he always had been, and now, just like that, he was gone. Snuffed out like he'd never existed.

It should have been me. He would regret stepping aside until the day he died.

Limbs were strewn about like puzzle pieces waiting to be put back together. Kell stumbled to his feet, clutching the rent in his side and struggling to draw breath. Screams drifted on the lazy breeze as it circled the fallen warriors, their leather armour in tatters and their faces a reflection of horror.

Kell's heart felt fit to burst from his chest and he cursed the mountains in the east, barely visible through the haze of black smoke. The rocky peaks winked at him, the crystals there scintillating coyly. They offered power, to be sure, but that power couldn't justify so many deaths, could it? Did it justify Mehdi's death? No. Nothing was worth that.

Humans were greedy beasts, more apt to destroy than create. They almost deserved the destruction of this day. Almost.

—Melissa Terry is a writer hailing from Toronto, Canada. She graduated from university with a Specialized Honours BA Theatre degree, then promptly sold out for a career in corporate banking. She's dabbled with blogging, podcasting, and reviewing (mainly horror) films, but is most passionate about writing speculative fiction. She lives with her husband and rescue dog, neither of whom listen to her.

Exercise Example 2, by Andy Dibble

Smelling the burning bodies was almost... good? It did smell good, savory. He was so hungry.

His master, back in Shravasti, had made some distinction between first and second order desires. His first order desire was to be a cannibal, serve his base needs. That desire was raw. It simply was. But he had a second order desire too, a reaction to the first, shame, disgust, wanting not to want to eat the only food available to him—human flesh.

Just think about the vermin, the rot that would set in, the muck and bad air hovering all around the heaped and charring flesh. Gods, he still so wanted to eat! What else? There would be alchemists' draughts too, draining from the sieges works— temperamental yellow, noxious green—mingled with the bodies. Those could dissolve his throat, his stomach, searing gaping wounds in his insides.

He no longer wanted to eat.

—Andy Dibble is a former academic and Sanskritist turned healthcare IT consultant. He lives near his hometown in southern Wisconsin, but has supported the electronic medical record of large healthcare systems in six countries. His fiction also appears in *Writers of the Future* and *Sci Phi Journal.* You can find him at andydibble.com.

About the Contributors

Franco Amati
Author, "Vat Life"
Franco Amati is a speculative fiction writer from New York. His educational background is in cognitive science. His fiction has appeared in *The Colored Lens, Stupefying Stories, Utopia Science Fiction*, and other places. You can find more of his work at www.francoamatiwrites.com.

Brian C.E. Baker
Artist, "Scott Thrower Profile Picture"
Brian lives with his wife, son, and two cats in Cleveland Heights, Ohio. While primarily a self-taught painter and sculptor, his early education was in architectural stone carving under Master Carver, Bob Ragan of Texas Carved Stone in Florence, Texas. Brian studied at the University of Saint Francis in Fort Wayne, Indiana in 2006, and the Pennsylvania Academy of the Fine Arts in Philadelphia, from 2010 – 2011. He can be found online at www.bcebaker.net.

Maureen Bowden
Author, "Nominative Determination"
Maureen Bowden is a Liverpudlian living with her musician husband in North Wales. She has had 132 stories and poems accepted for publication, she was nominated for the 2015 Pushcart Prize and in 2019 Alban Lake published an anthology of her stories *Whispers of Magic*. She loves her family and friends, rock 'n' roll, Shakespeare and cats.

Victoria Feistner

Author, "Turtle Hatchlings"

Victoria Feistner is a writer, a graphic designer, and an artisan, in equal parts—although some parts are more equal than others. She resides in Toronto with her partner and two ~~jerks~~ cats. Examples of her writing can be found at www.victoriafeistner.com.

M.X. Kelly

Author, "Star Trip(tych)"

M.X. lives in St. Petersburg, Florida with her partner, Val, their two cats, and a coffee pot. Her work has appeared in *Star*Line*, *Abyss & Apex*, *Scifaikufest*, *Queer Sci-Fi* and other magazines and anthologies across the known 'verse. M.X.'s website can be summoned with the typed incantation of http://mxkelly.weebly.com/.

Erin Kirsh

Author, "Witching"

Erin Kirsh is a writer and performer from Vancouver. A Pushcart Prize nominee, her work has appeared in dozens of lit journals including *The Malahat Review*, *Arc Poetry Magazine*, *CV2*, *EVENT*, *PULP Literature*, *Maudlin House*, *Geist*, and *The Molotov Cocktail* where she won their *Shadow Award* for poetry. Visit her at www.erinkirsh.com or follow her on twitter @kirshwords.

Jeremiah Kleckner

Author, "Not a Vampire"

Jeremiah Kleckner has taught English/Language Arts in Perth Amboy since 2005. During that time, he earned the Samuel E. Shull Middle School's 2014/2015 Teacher of the Year award, wrote dozens of short stories, and self-published several books. Jeremiah lives in Jersey City with his wife, daughter, and an ever-increasing number of dogs and cats.

Avra Margariti
Author, "Bathwater Mermaid"
Avra Margariti is a queer Social Work undergrad from Greece. She enjoys storytelling in all its forms and writes about diverse identities and experiences. Her work has appeared in *Vastarien, Daily Science Fiction, Lackington's, Arsenika,* and other venues. You can find her on twitter @avramargariti.

John Mavin
Author, "Restraint"
A past nominee for both the *Aurora Award* and the *Journey Prize,* John Mavin is the author of *Rage.* He's taught creative writing at Capilano University, Simon Fraser University, the University of British Columbia, with *New Shoots,* and at the Learning Exchange in Vancouver's Downtown Eastside. Visit him at www.johnmavin.com.

Brian Rappatta
Author, "To Sift the Sacred"
Brian Rappatta hails from the American Midwest, though is currently living the expat life in South Korea. His short fiction in various genres has appeared in venues such as *Chilling Ghost Stories* from *Flame Tree Publications, Shock Totem, Writers of the Future,* and *Amazing Stories,* as well as in various podcasts such as *Tales to Terrify* and *Gallery of Curiosities.*